The Adventures of
Thomas Pilgrim and
Barney High Tail

By

Henry L. Hixson

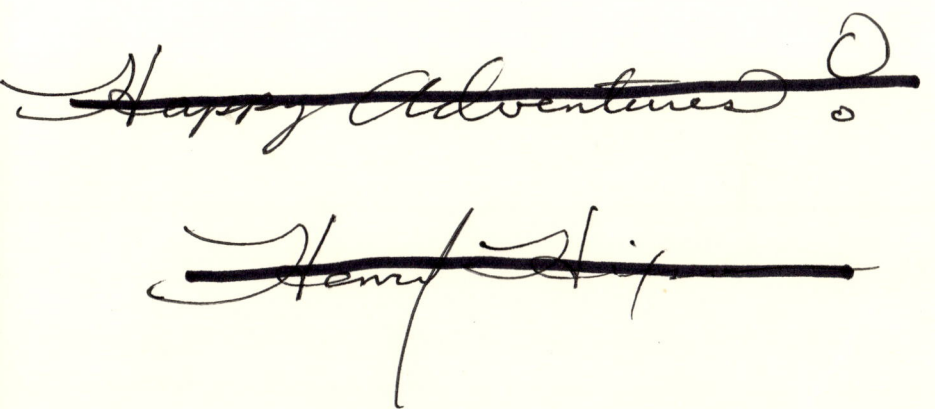

Copyright © 2010. Henry Hixson.
All rights reserved.
ISBN: 1452898278
ISBN-13: 9781452898278
LCCN: 2010907931

Acknowledgments

My heart felt thanks go to all those who encouraged and assisted me in writing this book, especially to my wonderful wife Sharon. Who had to endure untold hours of questions, but was still able to keep our marriage intact. Thanks to the staff of CreateSpace for their patience and understanding of my computer illiteracy. To Natalie Northcott for taking an old fashioned, hand written document, and creating a legible manuscript. Also to Bruce Vander Heide for his computer "know how". I'll never tell him again that he spends too much time in front of the screen. Last, but not least, thanks to my illustrator Paula Veschore, for her life like and detailed illustrations. To all of you I give my sincere thanks.

The Adventures of
Thomas Pilgrim and Barney High Tail

By

Henry L. Hixson

The Adventures of
Thomas Pilgrim and Barney High Tail

By

Henry L. Hixson

The year was 1795 and the place was a small English seacoast town where thirteen-year-old Thomas Pilgrim lived with his mother, father, sister, and his special friend, a cat named Barney High Tail. Thomas's mother worked at home doing the daily chores of preparing meals and cleaning the house while his father worked as a shipbuilder on the nearby docks. Thomas's younger sister, Robin, helped their mother with the inside chores while Thomas worked outside, keeping the small yard clean and splitting the wood scraps that he hauled back from the ship building yard where his father worked.

Day after day, Thomas made the trip with his wheelbarrow down the stone street to the docks. Quite often, Barney High Tail the cat would accompany Thomas, getting a free ride in the wheelbarrow. However, on the return trip, Thomas would try to encourage Barney High Tail to walk because of the heavy load and steep incline up the street. After arriving back home, Thomas would stack the smaller pieces and split the larger ones. The wood was always a welcome sight because the family used it to heat the house and cook the meals. Although this was a chore for Thomas, he enjoyed the trip to the docks because he could see his father working and he found the ships intriguing. So each afternoon, Thomas would take his wheelbarrow, along with his friend Barney High Tail, and head down to the docks.

Thomas collected wood scraps late in the afternoon, just as the builders were finishing for the day. This was a good time because the wood scraps were plentiful, and Thomas would not be in the way of the builders. Thomas's dad, having witnessed several accidents, had always cautioned Thomas about the danger of getting too near the ships. If Thomas and Barney High Tail ever arrived early on the docks, Thomas would lean against a piling and whittle on little wood scraps while waiting for the ship builders to complete their daily tasks. Thomas enjoyed carving small ships and cats. He would often use Barney High Tail as a model, along with a beautiful cat necklace that his grandmother Memaw had given him. This special cat had tiger eye stones for eyes and was one of a kind. Thomas's carving talent was so good that many of the ship builders would stop and admire his work.

One afternoon, as Thomas sat watching the work being done on a large sailing ship, he decided to try something new. He would not only whittle a ship, but it would be just like the one his dad was building. It would have every detail the real ship had, including the three tall masts, complete with sails and cargo. As he carved away on the little ship, Thomas would often show Barney High Tail and say, "Barney High Tail, let's go sail."

As Thomas watched the building progress of the large ship, he started to wonder what the name of this beautiful ship would be, what cargo it would carry, and where it would sail.

One night as Thomas was having supper with his family, he said, "Dad, tell me about the huge sailing ship you are now building. It's the biggest ship I've seen in the boatyard. I can't believe the height of the masts."

"It's definitely a big one," Mr. Pilgrim replied. "It's a three-massed square-rigged frigate that is being fitted to carry lots of cargo."

"What kind of cargo will it carry?"

"I don't really know at this time. The manifest is not complete, but I've heard it will be a lot. As you can see, some of the cargo is already being stored on the dock, ready to be loaded."

Thomas knew that manifest meant cargo because he had heard several of the other builders discussing it the day before. About that time, Robin said with a laugh, "Looks like you have a lot of cargo left on your plate, and if you don't hurry up and clean it, Mom and Dad may set you sailing."

Thomas laughed and continued eating. "What about her name, Dad? Does she have one? Since you have helped build so many, wouldn't it be nice if they named her after you? I know, we could name her after Barney. She could be called The Barney Boat."

Mr. Pilgrim answered with a smile, "Let's see, I think she's going to be called The Clean Plate Queen," and then he laughed. "Not really, Thomas. They haven't named her yet, and have just started to advertise for a crew to sail her. How would you like to be one of the crew that sails her on the maiden voyage? I think it would be fun and exciting, but I would sure miss being at home. Well, you're a little young now, Thomas, but maybe one day you will have a chance to sail on one of these ships."

Friends and Foes

While not going to school or doing his daily chores, Thomas would often play with his friend Christopher who lived down the street. Christopher's dad also worked at the docks with Thomas's father, and, like Thomas, the ships were always intriguing to Christopher.

One afternoon, as Thomas and Christopher were returning from a friend's house, they noticed a poster on a lamppost. The poster noted that the English Admiralty was asking for volunteers to sail on the new ship their fathers were building. It mentioned a sign-up date for the new crew, and also the ship christening ceremony the following month. Thomas and Christopher discussed how much fun it would be to be a sailor aboard the new ship, but realized they would have to wait a few years before that consideration.

As they continued their walk back to Christopher's house, they approached a tavern called Pelican Pete's Pub. This was a very popular meeting place for sailors and such. As Thomas and Christopher got near the pub, the front door swung open and out stumbled two drunken sailors. Thomas and Christopher stopped immediately to keep from bumping into them, as the sailors stepped out into the street and yelled at the lads. Arm in arm, the sailors staggered down the street just ahead of the boys. The lads were careful not to get too close, but were close enough to hear parts of their conversation, some of which they could not repeat.

That evening, Thomas told his mother and father about what had happened, and that he and Christopher had heard some of the conversation between the two sailors. Thomas's dad asked what the sailors looked like.

"Scary," said Thomas. "They both looked like pirates! One had long black hair and a monkey on his shoulder. The other one had a big scar on his face and glaring blue eyes."

"What did they have to say?" Mr. Pilgrim inquired.

"Other than cursing and telling us to get out of their way, not much else was said, except something about getting their next ship. After we got cursed at, Christopher and I really tried to let them get way ahead of us. Dad, do you know who those sailors are?"

"I don't know them, but I have heard their names are Kelly Brogdon and Jack Curt." Mr. Pilgrim, not being one to say anything bad about anyone, just said, "If you see those two again, try to avoid being in their presence."

Later, Christopher's dad shared a little more information with the boys. The two sailors they had run into were known as "Bad Brogdon" and "Cutlass Curt" by the other sailors. Knowing that Christopher's dad was more willing to discuss the matter, Thomas asked him how they got their names.

"Well, it's only hearsay," he said, but he had heard that both sailors were once buccaneers and were known around town as ruffians. Thomas knew that "ruffian" meant someone who showed bad behavior, but was not exactly sure about the word "buccaneer."

Christopher immediately replied, "A buccaneer is a pirate!"

Thomas now knew why the sailors looked the way they did, and could only imagine how Cutlass Curt had received his scar.

The Ceremony and Crew

A month later, the ship's construction was almost complete. There continued to be a lot of activity about the ship and on the docks. Thomas had been busy as well with his carvings of little cats and ships.

The next day was the christening ceremony of the new ship. The ceremony would include reading the names of the crew that would sail her on the maiden voyage.

That evening, Thomas said, "Why don't I try and sell some of my carvings at the ceremony tomorrow?"

Thomas's mom and dad thought it was a great idea. However, Robin chuckled and said, "Who would want to buy those little carvings?"

Thomas replied, "Everyone that I show them to." He laughed. He could hardly sleep that night for thinking about the opportunity to sell his carvings.

The next day came, and the excitement was growing around town. With Barney perched atop his wheelbarrow filled with carvings, Thomas and his family left for the ceremony. As they got closer to the docks, bands could be heard playing and people were everywhere. Some were selling stew, sweet bread, cookies, and drinks. Thomas wondered if the people would have any money left to purchase his carvings.

Thomas's dad suggested that they stand near the back so people would pass by Thomas after the ceremony. This would give him a chance to show more people his carvings. Thomas thought this was a great idea.

The ceremony began with the mayor welcoming everyone and thanking the shipbuilders for doing such a good job. Thomas's and Christopher's dads along with the other shipbuilders were recognized for their part in the shipbuilding. Everyone clapped and yelled when all of the builders were asked to come forward and be recognized. Special monetary awards were given to the builders for completing the ship on time.

As the festivities continued, the mayor announced that Admiral Dudley would read the names of the newly formed crew that would make the maiden voyage. It would be approximately one hundred and twenty-five men, somewhat fewer than would normally be on a sailing ship of this size.

Admiral Dudley began reading the names of the crew in alphabetical order, and requested that each stand and be recognized as his name was called. As he got to the last names that began with the letters B and C, something strange happened.

The admiral said, "The next crew members are Kelly Brogdon and Jack Curt."

About that time, Christopher looked at Thomas and whispered, "Aren't those the two sailors our fathers said to stay away from?"

"Yes," replied Thomas, "and, based on how they were acting, I can understand why they are known as *Cutlass Curt* and *Bad Brogdon!*"

"With their reputations, maybe they should not be crew members," whispered Christopher.

"I agree," Thomas said quietly, "but it's a little late now."

After the reading of the crew members, the admiral then announced, "I guess all of you are now wondering, why such a small crew for such a large ship? The reason is that this great sailing ship, the name of which will be given shortly, will carry additional cargo with fewer crew members. It was built and fitted for a special purpose. As all of you know, the HMS *Venture*, under the command of Captain Gates, sailed from this port approximately one year ago to Tahiti in the South Pacific. The *Venture* and its fine crew have not been heard from since. Because of the concern for its whereabouts, the English throne has requested that the maiden voyage of this ship be to locate the *Venture*, and, with God's blessing, resupply her for the trip back home. This mission will take the leadership skills of an experienced captain. It gives me great pleasure to present Captain Flowers."

Captain Flowers thanked the mayor, admiral, and other dignitaries, and said, "I am proud to announce that our crew was totally filled by volunteers.

The Ceremony and Crew

Not a single man had to be pressed into service. This shows the concern that each of these men have for Captain Gates and the crew of the *Venture*. I would like to now introduce to you the officer and crew. Mr. Douglas will serve as First Mate and Mr. Christian will serve as Boatswain. I have the utmost confidence that with our fine crew, under the leadership of these good men, we will find Captain Gates and the crew of the *Venture*."

Upon learning this, the entire crowd cheered and clapped. Then, Admiral Dudley said, "I would like to have Queen Dianna come forward for the christening."

As Queen Dianna approached the platform, sailors on each side of the ship readied their axes to cut the lines holding the ship in place. Queen Dianna said in an elevated voice, "I am proud to christen you the HMS *Provider*," at which time she broke a bottle upon the bow of the ship.

At that moment, the ship lines were cut and the huge ship began sliding down into the water. The crowd began cheering and clapping as the HMS *Provider* crashed into the water and settled into its berth.

Admiral Dudley then announced that all who would like could come aboard the HMS *Provider* for a visit. When Thomas and Christopher heard this, they immediately ran through the crowd to ask their parents if they could go aboard the ship. Both parents agreed, but Thomas's dad told Thomas to try and make it back to where he would attempt to sell his carvings.

Thomas and Christopher worked their way through the crowd and happened to be two of the first to board the ship. As they stepped across the gangplank onto the main deck, they were greeted by Captain Flowers, First Mate Douglas, and Boatswain Christian. Captain Flowers said proudly, "Welcome aboard the HMS *Provider*, lads!"

Thomas and Christopher were so eager they didn't know where to start. Then, Thomas said in an excited voice, "Our dads helped build this ship!"

Boatswain Christian replied, "And what a great job they did in building it! Oh, by the way, are you the lad that I have seen carving away on the docks?"

"Yes, sir, that's me. My name is Thomas Pilgrim, and this is my friend, Christopher."

Admiral Dudley said, "May I have everyone's attention! I almost forgot one of the most important announcements. That is, when will the HMS *Provider* set sail? Because of this trip, the HMS *Provider* will set sail two weeks from today. After today's ceremony, we will begin completing the final touches on our ship and will start loading cargo in one week."

Upon hearing that, Thomas said, "Let's hurry up and walk around the ship before the crowd comes aboard."

"Good idea Thomas, and hopefully we won't run into those two sailors."

The Ship

When Thomas and Christopher started walking around the main deck, they could not help but notice the size and height of the three huge masts that protruded up from the main deck. They could only imagine what the sails would look like when filled with wind. As Thomas gazed up, the main mast seemed to link the ship with the winter clouds above.

As Thomas and Christopher stepped up on a higher deck, Thomas said, "This is the quarterdeck, where the helm is."

"That's right," First Mate Douglas said. "Would you care to try your hand at the helm, mate?" the First Mate asked.

"Aye, aye, sir!" Thomas replied.

"A little more leeward lad. Now, steady as she goes."

Thomas thought, *this would be great if we were actually sailing on the sea.*

About that time, Thomas could see Christopher climbing up some of the rigging and heard First Mate Douglas say, "Careful, lad! Don't slip on those ratlines! Better come down, lad; these decks are mighty hard to fall on."

As Christopher began climbing down, Thomas noticed all of the people pouring aboard the ship. "Thomas, let's go below decks and check out the big guns."

It suddenly dawned on Thomas what his father had said about getting back quickly to sell his carvings. "Christopher, we don't have enough time.

We'll have to come another day. Let's get back so I can sell some of my carvings."

Getting across the gangplank was like being two fish swimming upstream.

"Careful, Christopher," Thomas said, "that water is mighty cold."

The Carvings

A few minutes later, Thomas and Christopher made it back through the crowd, and Thomas thanked his dad for watching over his carvings. Thomas immediately started carefully removing his carvings from the wooden crate that was in his wheelbarrow. "I think I'll flip the crate over and use it to display my carvings," said Thomas.

"Good idea, Thomas, let me give you a hand."

No sooner had Thomas begun placing his carvings on the crate than people started coming by and noticing them.

"Are these for sale?" one person asked.

"Yes sir. I just have not had a chance to get out my For Sale sign," answered Thomas.

"How much?" asked a woman.

"Uh, just whatever you could give me," Thomas replied.

"They are just beautiful, and so life like," said the woman, as she handed Thomas several silver coins.

"Thank you ma'm! Would you like a ship or a cat?"

"I think a ship," replied the woman. "I really like your cats, but since this is the celebration day for the HMS *Provider* and her crew, maybe the ship would be better."

As the word spread and more people noticed, Thomas and Christopher got really busy. Although Thomas had started with a crate full of carvings, he was now down to only one ship and the special cat, which was not for

15

sale. This special cat that hung on Thomas's neck was the one that his grandmother Memaw had given him. It was also special because it looked exactly like his friend Barney High Tail. It was solid black, with beautiful tiger eyes and a long tail that stood straight up. The tiger eye stones had been given to his Memaw by his grandfather Henry. Not only special, this was a sentimental cat.

As afternoon approached, Christopher said to Thomas, "I'd better be getting home now."

Thomas replied, "Yeah, I guess I'd better start to close up shop now as well. Thanks again, Christopher, for your help today. Why don't I share some of the profit with you?"

"Don't worry about it, Thomas. I was glad to be of help."

"Well, why don't you at least take this one last ship?"

"Okay, Thomas, that's a deal. As a matter of fact, I was hoping you would give me one. Thanks very much. I'll sail on home and probably see you tomorrow."

"Okay, Christopher, thanks again for your help."

As Christopher turned and walked away, Thomas could see two men approaching from the opposite direction. As they drew closer, he suddenly noticed it was Bad Brogdon and Cutlass Curt. Remembering what his father had said about these two, Thomas tried not to make eye contact with them. The closer they got, the faster Thomas tried to pack everything up. Too late; the two stopped abruptly in front of Thomas as he hurried to put away his sign.

"Carvings for sale, eh?"

"Well…well, not really, sir. You see, I did have some, but I just ran out and I've got to get home," replied Thomas.

"Ran out?" Brogdon said loudly.

"Yes, sir," Thomas replied in a quivering voice. "I had ship and cat carvings, but I sold them all."

"Cat carvings like the one you have around your neck?" Cutlass Curt said, as he glared down at Thomas.

"Yes, sir," said Thomas.

"Well, you ain't exactly run out, are ya?" Brogdon growled.

"Yes sir. I mean, no, sir. This one is not for sale. You see, this one was given to me by my grandmother Memaw. It has the tiger eyes, and I use it as a pattern to carve the others. Also, it brings me good luck."

The Carvings

"Special, eh? Let's take a closer look at it to see what's so special, lad."

Thomas was so scared he could hardly speak. "Sir...sir, I...I really have to be going home now."

"What's the matter, lad, cat got your tongue?" Bad Brogdon said with a smirk on his face. Brogdon then leaned over, pulling the necklace close to his face. "You'll be going home after I take a closer look at this cat!" He was so close that Thomas could smell his hot, bad breath, which reminded him of Pelican Pete's Pub. "Take it off so I can get a better look," Brogdon demanded.

Thomas was so scared now, he could hardly move. *Should I run?* Crossed Thomas's mind. *And if I did, would they catch me, and then what?* Although shaking and reluctant to remove the cat, Thomas knew it was the only way he would be able to safely leave.

"Let's see it, and let's see it now!" Brogdon said with a determined voice..

As he slowly removed the chain from around his neck, Thomas knew that he was in the presence of two very bad men, and the only way out was to do what they said.

"What's the cat's name?" Brogdon inquired.

"I...I call him Barney High Tail, after my cat, Barney," answered Thomas.

"I like his eyes," Cutlass Curt said, as he glared down at Thomas.

"Well, lad, this is the one I want!" Brogdon declared.

"No sir. No sir! As I said, it's not for sale," said Thomas.

"What's your name, lad?" growled Brogdon.

"Thomas Pilgrim, sir," answered Thomas.

"Well, Thomas Pilgrim, it's like this, my lad...everything has a price, even you and your cat Barney High Tail. Some things are bought and some things are taken. I'm willing to buy this cat for, let's say, this much." Brogdon reached in his pocket and pulled out several gold coins.

Thomas could not believe his eyes. "Is that real gold?" he asked.

"Argh, 'tis real gold, and much more than old Barney is worth!"

Thomas began to think about all he could purchase with the gold coins, and thought, *I could always carve another one.* "Okay," Thomas said in a reluctant voice, "I guess I'll sell it to you."

"I thought you would see it my way," replied Brogdon.

No sooner had Thomas put the coins in his pocket and watched the two men walk away than an empty feeling suddenly came over him. Thomas then realized what he had just done, and tried to justify his actions by saying to himself, "I can carve another Barney High Tail." Then, reality set in. "I don't have any tiger eye stones! What will grandmother Memaw and my parents think? I believe I've just made a bad decision."

Gold for Soul

Although Thomas had made good money on the sale of his carvings, he was still trying to justify having sold his prized possession. The trip home gave him time to really ponder on what he had done. As Thomas entered his home, he was greeted by Robin at the door.

"Well, Thomas, how did you do?"

"I sold them all and made lots of money!" said Thomas.

"You did?" replied Robin. "That's great, how much?"

Hearing the conversation, Thomas's dad said, "That's good news. Have you counted your profits?"

"Not yet, but I've got a lot to count."

With both pockets filled, Thomas reached into one and pulled out a fistful of coins. "See how much I made!" Thomas said in an excited voice, as one of the gold coins fell to the floor.

"What's this, gold? Not that they are not worth it, but someone gave you gold?" asked Thomas's father.

"Yes sir. I mean, it was worth it," replied Thomas.

Thomas's dad immediately noticed that Thomas was not wearing his Memaw's necklace. "Which carving did you sell for the gold coins?"

"Well, it was actually not one of the carvings…," said Thomas.

"Wait, let me guess," said Thomas's dad. "You sold your Memaw's good luck necklace? Tell me you didn't. I know it was yours, son, but why did you sell it?"

Looking down at the floor, Thomas knew he should not have sold the necklace. With his eyes filling with tears, Thomas began to cry as he ran to his room.

As Thomas lay on his bed sobbing, he knew that he had done a terrible thing, but did not know how to rectify it. After discussing the matter, Thomas's mom and dad knocked on his door and asked if they could talk with him.

"Thomas," Mrs. Pilgrim said, "your dad and I are very proud of you for having sold all of your beautiful carvings. We both know how much time it took for you to carve them. But we both thought that you would have wanted to keep your Memaw's necklace. It was so special to all of us."

"I know," Thomas replied. "I just got scared!"

"Scared?" Mr. Pilgrim said. "Scared of what?"

"Scared of the man I sold it to," Thomas replied.

"What did he do to scare you, Thomas? Did he take Memaw's necklace from you?"

"No, Dad, not exactly," answered Thomas.

"Then what do you mean, not exactly, Thomas?" his father asked.

"Well, I was scared of everything—the way they looked down at me, and the way they talked just scared me," said Thomas. "They even said that I could not leave until I showed them the necklace."

Seeing that Thomas was really upset about what had happened, his mom put her arms around him and said, "Thomas, its okay. We know in our hearts how you must feel, and we know that Memaw would have forgiven you. Now, let's count your money and see how much you've made."

"Thanks, Mom. I'll separate the gold coins that Mr. Brogdon and Mr. Curt gave me," said Thomas.

"So it was those two sailors who intimidated you? Is that correct?" asked Thomas's father.

"Yes, Dad, but I didn't go up to them. They came to me when I was getting ready to leave and I couldn't get away. They insisted that I sell them Memaw's necklace. I remembered what you said, Dad, about not being in the presence of those two sailors, but I was so scared. I could not move. I wanted to run, but I was scared they would catch me before I could get away. I hope I never see them again."

"I believe you, Thomas. I guess I'm just disappointed that you no longer have Memaw's necklace."

"I know, Dad. If I had it to do all over again, I would not have let them scare me into selling it," Thomas said.

"I understand, son, and I think we've all learned a lesson from this. Who knows, maybe one day we will get it back."

Later that evening, after the children had gone to bed, Thomas's mom and dad discussed the events of the day. Both agreed that Thomas had made a bad decision, but Thomas's dad was not ready to forget how Thomas had been coerced into selling Memaw's necklace.

Cargo

One week left and the loading of cargo had begun. It seemed as though the more cargo that was loaded, the more curious Thomas got. What was in those large barrels, boxes, and bottles? His curiosity rose even more with the different aromas. One aroma reminded him of his mother's fresh baked bread, and another of fish.

That evening at supper, Thomas asked his father about the cargo.

"Well, Thomas, what kind of food would you take on a long voyage like this?" asked his father.

"Mom's bread, beans, sweet cake, and milk," Thomas replied.

"Except for the milk, Thomas, I know the ship will be carrying bread, hardtack, dried beef, dried fish, dried vegetables, fruit, molasses, oatmeal, lots of water, and probably some other types of food and beverage. One thing it will not be carrying is all the cannons and gunpowder it would normally have."

"Sounds like with all that food, there won't be much room left for anything else," replied Thomas.

"It looks that way. But it will have twelve cannons, which is about half as many as a ship this size would normally have. It's going to be a long voyage, and hopefully there will be enough food and they will not need the extra cannons. Twelve should be a sufficient amount in the capable hands of Captain Flowers."

About that time, several men rolled a leaking barrel by.

"I've smelled that before, but I can't remember where," said Christopher.

"I have too," answered Thomas, "and I think it's either Pelican Pete's Pub or Bad Brogdon's breath."

Hatching the Plan

Three days left and the loading had reached an incredible pace. Because of all the excitement, Christopher was allowed to visit Thomas at the dock, but with the understanding that they would not get in the way. Although both boys knew about most of the cargo, they could not recognize what was in some of the crates and barrels, and the aromas added to their curiosity.

Christopher asked, "Wouldn't it be exciting to sneak on board and see what everything is and where it is being stored?"

"It sure would," Thomas replied.

Christopher, with a sly grin, said, "I have a great idea! Let's sneak aboard one afternoon when all the workers have left for home. No one would know but you and me."

"I don't know, Christopher. Maybe it would not be exactly sneaking aboard if we didn't disturb anything," said Thomas.

"That's right, Thomas," said Christopher.

"Okay, but would our parents approve of that?" asked Thomas.

"I don't know. But do you think they would really mind if we went aboard for just a little while?" asked Christopher.

"Good question," said Thomas.

"I have another good idea," Christopher said. "Since the ship sets sail this Saturday morning, we could spend Friday night with each other and go aboard then."

"Wait a minute, Christopher, I'm confused. What does spending the night have to do with going aboard the ship?" asked Thomas.

"Well, Thomas, you see, I could be spending the night with you, and you could be spending the night with me. No one would know, and it would give us enough time to see the whole ship and spend the night on her," said Christopher.

"Wow, that would be great, Christopher. But we would have to be off the ship early Saturday morning before the crew arrives and they set sail," said Thomas.

"We can do that, Thomas," said Christopher.

"Okay, Christopher, let's check with our parents tonight and talk tomorrow about our final plans," said Thomas.

"Great idea, Thomas, but remember not to say anything about the ship. It's a secret, just between you and me," said Christopher.

That night at the supper table, Thomas inquired about the ship and its progress. "Well, Dad, I understand the ship will be leaving port this coming Saturday."

"That's correct, Thomas. It's fully loaded and ready to set sail. The only thing left is for Captain Flowers to say, *'All hands on board!'*" said Thomas's father.

"If its okay with you and Mom, Christopher has asked if I could spend Friday night with him, and we could walk down to the docks Saturday morning to see it sail," said Thomas.

"It's okay with me if your mom approves. Just remember, stay out of the way," said Thomas's dad.

"Thanks, Dad, we will be careful," said Thomas.

The next afternoon, Thomas met with Christopher at the docks to discuss their plan.

"Well, Thomas, are you ready to spend tomorrow night with me?" asked Christopher.

"Oh yeah! And are you ready to spend the night with me, Christopher?" asked Thomas.

Hatching the Plan

"I think so, Thomas. But what would our parents say if our plan didn't work and we had to get off the ship for some reason and go home?" asked Christopher.

"Don't worry, Christopher. Nothing is going to happen. But even if it did, one of us could have gotten a bellyache and had to go home. That way, our parents would not have to know about the ship, and would understand why we came home early."

"But, Thomas, wouldn't that be telling a story?" asked Christopher.

"I guess, Christopher, but I don't think we will get into trouble. Just don't worry about it. If we have to go home early, just make sure you have a real bellyache," laughed Thomas.

"I will, Thomas, but I still don't feel really good about it," Christopher said.

Sneaking on Board

It was late Friday afternoon and the sun was setting. All was quiet on the docks while the crew members were ashore enjoying their last evening before sailing the next day. Thomas arrived first at the docks, but was surprised to see that Barney High Tail had followed him. Knowing that he could not take Barney back home for fear of missing Christopher, Thomas decided to keep Barney with him. As he sat looking at the beautiful ship, he could only imagine what it would be like to sail aboard her. About that time, Christopher could be seen walking down the dock with what appeared to be a knapsack.

"Christopher, I thought at first you were one of the sailors with his duffel bag. What in the world did you bring?"

"Well, I have candy, water, and a blanket in case we get cold."

"I'm glad you brought them because I forgot to bring anything. It's just as well, because my parents would have asked why I was carrying a blanket to your house. How did you get out of your house with it?" asked Thomas.

"I told my parents that we might spend some time on the hill tonight watching the stars," said Christopher.

"Is that not *telling a story?*" asked Thomas.

"No, Thomas, because I said we *might* spend some time on the hill," replied Christopher.

"Oh, okay Christopher. Well, are you ready to go aboard the HMS *Provider?*" asked Thomas.

"Aye, aye, sir," Christopher replied.

"Since we have already seen the poop deck and quarterdeck, let's go see the gun deck first," Thomas suggested.

"Okay, Thomas. Maybe we can fire one of the cannons! Ha! Just kidding," joked Christopher.

As the boys and Barney started crossing the gangplank, Thomas whispered, "Be careful, Barney, that water is really cold."

The gangplank squeaked as the boys snuck aboard the ship. Well, here we are Christopher said with a voice of relief. As they weaved their way through the cargo, Christopher said, "Look, Thomas, here are the cannons. Look how big they are. But I only see six cannons on each side."

"That's right, Christopher. My dad said they needed the space to carry more food for the long voyage," said Thomas.

"But what would happen if they were attacked by pirates?" Christopher asked. "Do you think twelve cannons would be enough?"

"I don't know, but my dad says it is."

"Look, Thomas, here is another helm."

"Christopher, I don't think that's a helm. I think it's called a warping capstan."

"Did you say a warping captain?"

"No, I said a warping capstan."

"What's that?" asked Christopher.

"You know, it's the thing that rope is wound around so it can pull the ship closer to the dock when the sails are not up," explained Thomas.

"That would make sense, because you sure could not stop this big ship with all the sails up," Christopher said. "I wonder what's in this room, Thomas. Let's look inside."

As the boys opened the door, Thomas said, "This must be First Mate Douglas's cabin. Look at the maps and other stuff on the table. This is definitely not Captain Flower's cabin, because his probably has windows."

"I bet you're right, Thomas, and I bet I know where it is. Follow me," said Christopher.

When the boys got to the captain's cabin, they discovered that the door was locked. "Oh, well, Thomas, we've got plenty of other spaces to explore. Why don't we go down this hatchway and try to find the cargo holds and crew quarters?" Christopher suggested.

Sneaking on Board

As Thomas, Christopher, and Barney started down the ladder, the aroma of different foods permeated the air.

"We must be near the food storage area. Something smells really good," Thomas whispered.

"I know," replied Christopher, "and I am getting hungry. The only thing I brought was cookies."

As the boys sat eating their snacks, Barney was busy sniffing all the containers.

"Look, Thomas, I see a box that has been opened. I wonder if a rat did it," said Christopher.

"I hope not," replied Thomas. "What's inside it?"

"Oh, look, its hardtack. Since it is already opened, do you think they would mind if we ate a couple?" asked Christopher.

"Well, there are so many boxes, I don't think they would mind," replied Thomas.

As the boys sat eating the hardtack, Christopher said, "Look, Thomas, there's another opened box. Either there's a smart rat aboard, or someone else."

"Let's not think about that, Christopher. Let's just see what it is," said Thomas.

As Thomas looked into the container, Barney jumped down from a deck beam and landed on top of the container lid. Thomas screamed as he fell backward over a barrel, knocking over the container and spilling some of the dried fish that was in it. Christopher could not help but laugh as Barney began to eat one of the dried fish.

"We know what food Barney likes the best," said Christopher.

"I can see why," Thomas said, as he sampled a piece of dried fish with his hardtack.

As the boys sat finishing up their snacks and cleaning up the spilled food, they noticed an area across the deck that was fenced in.

"Look, Thomas, this must be a space for cows or something. There sure is a lot of hay. This is where I would like to sleep," said Christopher.

"Me to Christopher, but without the cow" You know, we have been aboard the ship for several hours now, and I could just curl up in the hay next to that barrel and take a nap," said Thomas. "But let's go forward and find out where the crew sleeps."

As the boys passed by another group of barrels, they could not help but notice a strong smell.

"What's that?" Christopher asked.

"Oh, that's cabbage," Thomas replied.

"I'm glad they have other kinds of food," said Christopher.

"That's true, but if you were on board you would have to eat this," said Thomas.

"You would? Thomas, may I ask why?" asked Christopher.

"My dad said it would help you not to get scurvy," answered Thomas.

"What's scurvy?" asked Christopher.

"I don't know, Christopher, but I think it's a disease that you get when you don't eat your vegetables," answered Thomas.

"Maybe I could mix the cabbage with molasses and put it on a hardtack," said Christopher.

"I don't know how that would taste, but it's good that we don't have to try it," Thomas said.

Other Guests Aboard

More than two hours had passed, and the boys were beginning to get a little tired. As they reached the crew's quarters, both welcomed the hammocks which were stretched between the beams directly in front of them.

"Boy, I sure could use some sleep. Let's get in a hammock and take a little nap," said Christopher.

"Sounds good to me, Christopher," Thomas said.

Barney must have been equally tired, since he snuggled next to Thomas. Much to his surprise, Christopher fell sound asleep while Thomas lay awake thinking about the captain's cabin and how they might get in. Thomas then leaned over to Barney and said, "Barney, let's you and I leave Christopher asleep and go back to see if we can get into the captain's quarters to look around. If we can, we'll come back quickly to get Christopher."

As Thomas and Barney started making their way back aft with a dimly lit lantern, they passed a group of barrels that had a familiar smell. Thomas paused and said, "I've got it. That's the same thing we smelled when we passed Pelican Pete's Pub. Since these barrels are so close to the hay, I don't know if I could sleep here or not."

After weaving their way through more barrels, crates, and other gear, Thomas and Barney finally made it to the stern of the ship. "Okay, Barney, one more ladder to climb, and this should put us near the captain's cabin," said Thomas. When they reached the last step on the ladder, Thomas's foot slipped, and he made a loud noise as he fell to the second step. "I'm sure glad I didn't drop our lantern." As he sat there for a minute with Barney, he could not help but wonder what Christopher would think if he woke up and discovered they were gone. "Maybe we should not have left him alone. Oh, well, let's get up and see what we can, Barney."

When Thomas stood up and took the final step, he and Barney were totally shocked by what happened. A sailor's face appeared! A face he would never forget. Thomas and Barney stood frozen in place as the scary sailor said in a snarling voice, "Now what do we have here? Stowaways, ye are?"

Thomas could not speak, but could only take a step backward. As he did, he knew the only thing to do was to run. Not thinking about the height of the ladder, Thomas made an awkward leap down all the steps. As he landed with a crash on the floor, he felt a terrible pain in his right foot. Thomas thought, *No time for pain now; we've got to get back to Christopher and get off this ship.* Barney seemed to understand what had just happened and started leading the way back to Christopher. Not knowing if the sailor was following them or not, Thomas and Barney ran with all their might. When they got back to Christopher, both were totally exhausted and could only fall onto the hammock where Christopher was still sleeping.

"Wake up! Wake up, Christopher! We've been caught!" said Thomas.

Christopher, having been startled by their approach, rose up and said, "What?"

"Yes, that's right, we've been caught," answered Thomas.

"By who?" asked Christopher.

"By that sailor. You know, the one with the big scar on his face," said Thomas.

"Thomas, have you been dreaming? Are you serious?" Christopher asked.

"Yes! I'll tell you about it later," said Thomas.

Christopher jumped from the hammock, and as the boys and Barney started to leave, Thomas took one step and fell down in excruciating pain.

"What's the matter, Thomas?" Christopher whispered.

"I fell and hurt my foot," answered Thomas.

"Here, let me help you," said Christopher.

"No, Christopher, if we run into that sailor again, it's going to be trouble for both for us. Since you were not discovered, why don't you go ahead and get off the ship as fast as you can. Barney and I will wait a little while and sneak off when the coast is clear and my foot is better," said Thomas.

Other Guests Aboard

"Shall I wait on the docks for you?" asked Christopher.

"No, I think we're going to have to use our backup plan and go home," said Thomas.

"Will you be okay, Thomas?" asked Christopher.

"Yes, I'll be fine. Just tell your parents you got a bellyache, and don't mention anything about my hurt foot. Oh, and Christopher, don't leave by way of the gangplank. That sailor could be watching," said Thomas.

"Then how will I get off?" asked Christopher.

"You'll have to crawl down one of the lines," answered Thomas.

"What? I'll never make it!" said Christopher.

"Yes, you can, Christopher! Anyway, would you rather take a chance on getting caught on the main deck or crawl down a line?" asked Thomas.

"I'll take the line. Let me leave you the blanket and water," said Christopher.

"Thanks, Christopher. I'll return the blanket tomorrow," said Thomas.

As Christopher crawled through the cannon hatch and onto the line, Thomas whispered one last thing, "I'll meet you at the docks tomorrow at noon to see our ship sail away."

Christopher looked up, and with a slight grin he whispered, "Aye, aye, matey."

No sooner had Christopher lowered himself down the line two feet than he heard a voice from above. Looking up and seeing the glowering face of that same sailor, Christopher was frightened beyond imagination.

"Leaving like a rat, ye are?" bellowed the sailor. "Ye better be glad ye didn't stick around. Be gone with you, and never set foot on this ship again, lad, or you will surely suffer the consequences!"

Thomas, hiding below the sailor, heard every word and kept silent. He knew the sailor probably thought Christopher was him, not knowing that they both were on the ship.

Christopher continued down the line hand over hand as fast as he could go. He was approximately halfway down when he noticed what he thought was a big knot in the line. As he got farther down the line, he noticed the knot was moving! *It's not a knot; it's the biggest rat I've ever seen, and it's coming toward me!* Hanging precariously by his hands, Christopher knew he had to make a decision quickly. *Do I try to crawl back up the line toward the ship, or do I keep crawling toward the rat in hopes that he will turn and go back down to the docks?*

37

In either case, Christopher knew he was between two rats, one on the ship and one on the line. Within a split second, it was like the large rat had read Christopher's mind. Turning and almost slipping from the line, the rat scurried down toward the docks, with Christopher in hot pursuit. After planting his feet on the dock, Christopher turned as the sailor stared after him and said, "Be glad the rat didn't get you, lad, but be gladder that I didn't!"

Upon hearing that, Christopher ran down the docks and away from the ship.

Back on Board

Having heard and seen Christopher's escape, Thomas sat hidden, scared, and in pain. His ankle was now twice its normal size and was not getting any better. He whispered to Barney, "I've got to lie down, Barney, and let my foot rest before we sneak off the ship." As Thomas quietly limped toward the hammocks, he said, "I can't lie down here. If the sailor comes down here, we'll get caught for sure! Come on, Barney, let's find a place to lie down and hide."

As Thomas limped through the cargo containers, he remembered the secluded area with hay that was located behind the barrels with the unusual smell. "Come on, Barney, let's try to get there as quietly and quickly as we can," said Thomas. After taking several steps, Thomas knew it would not be quickly, for he was in much pain. It seemed like it took forever for Thomas and Barney to make it back to the caged area, and the soft, thick hay was a welcome sight. Trying to remain as inconspicuous as possible, Thomas grabbed several big armfuls of hay and placed these behind the large barrels next to the bulkhead. Thomas noticed that the aroma of the fresh hay helped mask the smell of whatever was in the large barrels next to him.

After stretching out on the soft hay and pulling up the warm blanket, Thomas could not help but think about his own bed at home. As Barney snuggled up next to him, Thomas noticed the pain was not as bad. "Maybe if we just lie here for an hour, we will be able to sneak off," he said. Thomas and Barney drifted off to sleep in the warmth and softness of their makeshift bed.

Fear Awakening

Thomas did not realize how tired he was until he was awakened from his sleep by loud noises of movement and voices. As he opened his eyes and peeked out through the partially opened cannon hatch cover, he could not believe what he saw. It was a long line of sailors walking across the gangplank. *What time is it, and how long have I slept?* Thomas wondered. *More importantly, how will I now get off? Be calm. Just be calm. I know it's still dark, and I know the ship is not leaving before noon.* "Maybe the sailors are just bringing their duffel bags aboard, and will be leaving the ship to return at noon," he whispered to the cat. "In any case, Barney, we will be patient and make our move as soon as possible."

Realizing that he would have sufficient time before dawn to leave, Thomas went back to sleep. Suddenly, he was awakened by a loud yell, "Prepare to cast off!"

Wait a minute! No way! Thomas thought. *This ship is not getting ready to move!* When Thomas lifted the hatch cover, he was shocked to see that not only was the ship starting to move, but there was not a single line attached. Thomas could not believe what was happening. "What do I do?" Thomas asked himself. As the seconds ticked away, Thomas thought, *my only option is to jump off and try to swim back to the docks!* Seconds turned into minutes. As he opened the hatch to jump, Thomas suddenly stopped and said, "Oh no! I forgot about Barney!" Now gripped with total fear, Thomas had to make a critical decision: jump with Barney and try to swim, or drop Barney off the

41

ship and both try to make it. "I can't do it, I can't do it," sobbed Thomas, as he fell back into the hay. The ship was several hundred yards away from the docks as Thomas tried to quiet his sobbing.

Minutes passed as thoughts raced through his mind. "I know the ship is not leaving now because it's supposed to leave at noon today," he told the cat. "So, what is it doing? Maybe it's a trial run to make sure everything is okay. That's it, a trial run. We'll be back shortly, Barney, and I'll make sure you and I get off safely." Minutes seemed to fly by. Thomas took another quick look at the docks that were now further away. There was noise and activity on the ship all around them. Then, Thomas heard someone yell something that made his heart sink. "Raise the mainsail!" With that, Thomas felt the large ship roll slightly to the left as the brisk, cold wind filled her large sails. As the ship lurched forward, Thomas felt a huge lump in his throat and a lonely, empty feeling.

Hearing the Truth

The ship groaned in the heavy wind as the coast of England slowly faded into the distance. As the cold wind whistled around the cannon cover, Thomas was still uncertain as to whether the ship was on a trial run or not. In any case, the hay was warm and the food was enough to hold them until they returned, hopefully within a few hours. Barney snuggled close to Thomas, as if to offer assurance that everything would be alright.

Minutes turned into hours. Thomas was starting to be concerned because he had not felt the ship change direction. *What if?* Thomas was now wondering. *What if, for some reason, the ship is not going to return, what do I do?* No sooner had Thomas had this thought than footsteps and voices could be heard coming from one of the ladders above decks. As they got closer, Thomas peeked around the barrels and saw that one of the voices was that of First Mate Douglas, and that the other belonged to Boatswain Christian.

"Well, Boatswain, it's a good idea that we got under way before the storm came," said First Mate Douglas.

"You're right about that, sir. I know all of the people in town will miss the official departure, but I think the captain made the right decision to leave early. I think we will experience enough bad weather without bringing on more. Now let's make sure all of the cargo is secured and report back to Captain Flowers," said Boatswain Christian.

Thomas could not believe what he had just heard. Reality set in, and Thomas was in total disbelief. Shock and fear now consumed him. Shaking and quietly sobbing, Thomas clutched Barney. "What do we do now, Barney? I want to go home. I want my mom and dad!"

Barney looked at Thomas as if he knew exactly what Thomas had said and how he felt. After several agonizing hours, Thomas wondered if Christopher would tell his parents the truth. *Will I ever get back home? If I'm found aboard the ship, will I be tossed overboard?* Thomas thought. *If I surrender to the captain and tell the truth, maybe he will turn around and take me back, or maybe he will put us adrift. What are the odds of any of this happening? I don't know, but I do know that I want to go home.*

Lonely and Scared

It was late in the afternoon, and the HMS *Provider* was plowing through the cold North Atlantic heading on a south-southwest course. As Thomas and Barney remained hidden in their home away from home, Thomas was still uncertain about what to do since so much time had lapsed. Thomas decided not to surrender to the captain because of the fear of being set adrift. He knew that would lead to certain death in the frigid North Atlantic waters. The only option left was to remain hidden for as long as possible and try to stay alive until help arrived.

As Thomas and Barney lay there trying to stay warm, Thomas could not help but think of his earlier thoughts about sailing aboard this ship. "Well, Barney, I guess you have to be careful what you wish for. Let's now think about how we can stay alive. The water and food we had is gone. Wait a minute—we are surrounded by food and water. But how do we gain access to it without getting caught?"

No sooner had Thomas mentioned this to Barney than voices and footsteps were heard again. This time, the voices sounded strangely familiar. It was First Mate Douglas and Bad Brogdon!

"Brogdon, I want a lantern hung here to light the water barrels, but not too close to the hay. We don't want a fire aboard the *Provider*."

"Aye, aye, sir, and it would light up anyone who might take mind to get more than his share of water," said Brogdon.

"Yes, it would, Brogdon, but hopefully that won't happen," said Mr. Douglas.

As the two walked away, Thomas thought, *we will have to be extremely careful when the lantern is lit. A fire caused by me would surely mean death for us, even if the crew was able to put it out.* Thomas could hear another conversation going on in the next compartment, and he listened closely.

"The seas and winds will catch us tonight, mate. So, it's good we got under way a little early."

"Aye, and hopefully we can stay ahead of the storm," said another voice.

When Thomas heard this, he knew there was no turning back. He was now considered a stowaway, and that could mean death if he was caught.

Hungry and Sick

Nightfall was fast approaching, and the storm that was close behind had almost caught up with the ship. Although the wind was blowing almost aft, the huge ship was starting to roll with the heavy seas. Having felt hungry at one point, Thomas and Barney were now starting to feel a bit queasy. "It was okay, Barney, when I could see the horizon, but now it's almost dark, and the ship's movement is having an effect on me. Oh, Barney, I feel so sick! I think I'm going to throw up!" said Thomas.

Thomas covered his mouth, but knew that he had to open the gun cover quickly.

No sooner had Thomas pushed open the cover than he let it fly. Trying to muffle the sound with one hand and hold the cover open with the other was almost impossible. Having relieved himself of what little he had left in his stomach, Thomas sat there on his knees with the cold air and ocean spray blowing in his face. Just for a minute, Thomas felt somewhat better, but not well enough to think about eating anything. The distant shore had now faded away, and the only things seen ahead were the huge ocean swells that were moving the ship around like a leaf in a stream. As Thomas eased back down into the soft hay, he whispered to Barney, "Let's just try and get some sleep. Maybe tomorrow we will feel better." Barney looked up at Thomas as if to agree with everything he had said.

Early to Rise

It seemed that no time had passed before Thomas and Barney heard movement and voices above them. Thomas wondered, *did we sleep at all?* With no way to tell time, Thomas could only guess. The sun was starting to break over the horizon, and the seas had calmed considerably, which was a blessing.

"Barney," Thomas said, "today will be our planning day. First, we will finish the snacks we brought aboard the ship. My stomach feels better, and I believe I can keep something down." As Thomas looked into the food bag, he began to cry. Not only had Christopher brought food for himself, but also enough for Thomas and Barney. "What a great friend we have in Christopher. I sure miss him, and wish he was here with us. At least it would be easier to get through this ordeal. But let's not fret. Christopher would not like that." After finishing the snacks, Thomas was able to drink some water, and poured some into his cupped hand for Barney. "Well, Barney, it's now planning time. For us to continue to live on this ship, we will need food, water, and not to get caught. The food and water should not be difficult; however, getting caught could be a problem." Thomas thought, *although it may not taste like Mom's, we are surrounded by food. But, oh no! Would that not be stealing to take it?* Thomas knew that if caught stealing food from the crew it would probably mean severe punishment or death. "Barney, we have no other choice. If caught, maybe the crew will have mercy on us and not throw us overboard. Now, let's see about the water. I know, we can refill Christopher's empty water bottle at night, but how about you, Barney? There's no bowl or container for you. If only I had a block of wood, I could carve a bowl for you, but there's no time for that."

As Thomas sat thinking, he noticed a knot in the wood decking right near where Barney was sitting. "Let's see, Barney. If I can just pry out this knot with my knife, it would almost be like a small bowl!" Thomas worked feverishly to pry out the knot. "Yes, there it is Barney, a built-in bowl. Let's see if it works." Thomas took the remaining water in the bottle and poured it into the knothole. "Great said, Thomas". Except for a little that came out when the ship rolled, it worked fine. Barney seemed to adjust to his new built-in bowl. The use of his knife made Thomas think about his carvings and what he would be doing if back home. That's all it took for those lonely feelings to come over Thomas. "Oh, Barney, if only I had done what was right, we would not be in this predicament." Barney looked at Thomas as if to say, "I know, but we have to be patient until help arrives." As Thomas stared at Barney with teary eyes, he patted the cat on the head and said, "Barney, you are my only friend now, and I promise I will always take care of you, no matter what happens."

Timing

Although still feeling terribly lonely and scared, Thomas made it through the second night and next day without being discovered. He and Barney were able to crawl around the provisions to where the different food items were located. Thomas knew that, to lessen the chance of getting discovered, most of his movement would have to be done at night. One false move by either of them would mean detection and consequences.

Early that evening, Thomas began to feel the urge to use the bathroom. "It was easier when I could go through the gun cover, but it's now different. Its sit-down time, and nowhere to go!" explained Thomas. Thomas knew that if he went inside the ship he would surely be detected. "I know, Barney, I'll try to hold off until it gets dark, and I'll go through the gun cover." Barney gave Thomas a "how about me?" look. Thomas whispered, "Barney, I'm sorry, but you will have to find your own place. Don't try what I'm going to do." Thomas was able to hold off until it was completely dark. As the ship slightly rolled back and forth, it was almost like it was saying to Thomas, "I'll try to help you." When Thomas could not hold back the urge any longer, he quietly lowered his pants and proceeded to back into the gun hatch opening. One slip without holding on would mean a disastrous plunge backward into the cold North Atlantic waters—and death! As Thomas sat holding on to the inside opening, he knew that timing was also a factor. *If I can just wait until the ship rolls down toward the water, I should have a relatively easy time of*

51

it. However, if my timing is off, and I go while the ship is rolling the opposite direction, things will get messy. Really messy! Without knowing who might show up, or when, Thomas knew he had to finish his business quickly. Also, his hindquarters were starting to get really cold from the air and spray. As the ship rolled to the right and began the opposite roll, Thomas said to himself, "Now's my chance." The timing could not have been better, and Thomas finished his business and crawled back into his hiding place. "Ah! Another accomplishment today. Today! Wait a minute, what is today? Let's see, the ship left Saturday, so today is Monday. No, the ship left Friday night, so today must be Sunday." It suddenly dawned on Thomas that he was starting to lose track of time. Without a way to remember, he would not know what day it was or how long he had been away.

As Thomas instinctively felt his pockets, he said, "I don't have anything to write with, just a knife. Wait a second." Thomas knew what to do as he gazed at the bulkhead next to them. "I'll cut a notch in the wood for each day. That means I'll make two straight notches and one notch shaped like a cross to represent today, which is Sunday. I will then be able to know what day it is and the number of days we have been gone, based on the number of notches. Hopefully there won't be many!"

Third Night – First Fright

The third day went without a hitch. As a matter of fact, except for the periods of homesickness, it went as well as could be expected. Thomas was also able to locate a piece of scrap wood the night before and spent most of the day carving, as Barney stayed close at hand.

As Thomas pulled up a large handful of hay for his pillow, he could not help but think about his family and what they would be doing. "Mom probably prepared my favorite Sunday dish of chicken and dumplings." The longer he laid thinking, the sadder he got. "I know they miss me as much as I miss them. I just hope that we will somehow get back home soon. Barney, let's go and find us something to eat. It's been a long day, and I'm ready to fall asleep." Although Thomas was not doing much physical activity during the day to make himself tired, the constant tension and swaying of the ship had a definite tiring effect on both him and Barney. That night, Thomas was so tired he fell asleep while holding a piece of dried beef in the palm of his hand.

As Thomas drifted off, he dreamed of being back home and playing with his close friend Christopher. Later that night, his dreams carried him to one night when he and Christopher had spent the night on a nearby hill. They had lain on their backs watching shooting stars and Christopher had tickled Thomas's arm with a twig. Thomas laughed to himself in his sleep, but the tickling continued, except now it was felt on his face…to such an extent that he awakened and opened his eyes. It was all Thomas could do to hold back a bloodcurdling scream. Perched on his chest was a huge brown rat that apparently had smelled the dried beef in his hand. "Oh, no! Oh, no!" Thomas knew he was not dreaming, and he instinctively swung his arm, hitting the rat and sending it flying across the deck. Thomas immediately began feeling his chest, hands, and face to make sure the rat had not bitten him. Thomas knew that if that had occurred, he could come down with a terrible disease and death could follow.

As Thomas turned to check on Barney, he discovered that he was nowhere to be found. Later in the night when Thomas was able to fall back asleep, Barney returned and started to curl up next to him. Thomas felt Barney against his arm and immediately jumped, thinking it was the rat. The sudden movement startled Barney so much that neither Thomas nor Barney was able to sleep the remainder of the night. Thomas now knew to never fall asleep with food in his hand. It was another of many lessons to be learned aboard this ship.

Scavenging

A week later, Thomas and Barney had adjusted to their stowaway life as much as possible. The same routine occurred every day. Early to rise, eating what food was available from the night before, carving that day's notch, and spending quiet time with Barney. Nights were spent quietly searching for food and water. Thomas and Barney had learned that the best time for this was right after bedtime and after the crew had made its watch rounds. Although this movement within the ship's hold was dangerous, it had become somewhat intriguing for Thomas and Barney.

Each night offered a new adventure as to what different type of food might be discovered and tried. The trick was to get the food container open, the food removed, and the container closed while not being detected. Thomas and Barney learned the hard way one night about not securing a lid back on a crate. The following night, Thomas and Barney noticed the lid on one of the hardtack crates had been left open. As he went to shut it, their unexpected visitor, the huge brown rat, jumped out of the open container and scurried away. Thomas had to keep from yelling and running himself, and Barney was so surprised that he didn't respond like a cat should. With hearts pounding, Thomas and Barney could only sit there in amazement. Thomas whispered to Barney, "The next time that happens, I want you to catch that rat and I will take care of him."

Barney looked up at Thomas as if to say, "Who, me?"

Conniving

Ten days, and the hope of a quick rescue had dwindled away. The only good thing was that Thomas and Barney were no longer seasick. The weather had changed drastically. The seas were much calmer, and the cold North Atlantic was behind them.

In addition to carving and secretively playing with Barney during the day, Thomas enjoyed listening to the crew conversations that went on all around them. Everything was heard, from discussions about loved ones back home, to favorite pets, to adventures on the sea.

It was one of these overheard conversations that was a cause of wonderment and concern for Thomas. It occurred late one night during a duty watch change. This was the time that one crew member was assigned to take over the duties of another crew member when his watch ended. Thomas had experienced this number of times, but this particular night was different. The crew member that was on duty during the day was none other than Kelly Brogdon, better known as Bad Brogdon. His relief was Jack Curt, better known as Cutlass Curt. The usual duty change occurred at the same time every day, and the sailor assigned would walk through the below decks at different times during the night to make sure all was well. The theft of food and water was not a common occurrence, mainly because of the punishment one would receive if caught. A crew member walking through during the night would also lessen the chances of this happening. However, what if there was a wolf, or wolves, guarding the henhouse? Things could change, and they did.

"Well, how's ye old mate Mr. Curt doing this fine evening?" Brogdon asked.

"Except for being a little dry, my friend Mr. Brogdon, all is well."

"Aye, 'tis like the times we've had before, but never dry for long, ye remember," said Bad Brogdon.

"I do, Mr. Brogdon, and ye remember, then and now, what friends are for in times of need—or should I say in times of thirst," said Cutlass Curt.

"Indeed, I do, Mr. Curt, and ye remember the care we took in satisfying our thirst?" asked Bad Brogdon.

"How well I do, Mr. Brogdon, so maybe a little thirst quencher the old-fashioned way would be in order," stated Cutlass Curt.

"'Tis we can, Mr. Curt, but never forget the consequences if ye are caught. My lips remain sealed, except for the time we tap the barrel," said Bad Brogdon.

Thomas could barely see the two men looking around and then secretly drinking from the barrel. Thomas could not tell exactly what they were drinking, but the aroma was very much like what he and Christopher had smelled outside of Pelican Pete's Pub. He also surmised, based on their conversation, the two sailors were stealing from the crew's rations. Thomas thought how wrong that was, but how could he blame them when he was doing the same thing? *But mine is out of necessity, not greed*, Thomas thought. *But would it matter for any reason if you were caught? I think not. I hate to consider the consequences if anyone, including myself, were caught.*

José the Monkey

Twelve days had passed, and except for the fact that the weather continued to get better, nothing had changed. Thomas and Barney had adjusted well to their secret life aboard the HMS *Provider*. Both now knew when and where they could move within their confined space without being detected. The calmer seas had allowed Thomas to concentrate more on his carving and the ability to move further into the ship without being detected. The main concern now was not to get complacent as they ventured out. One afternoon while Thomas and Barney were on a hide-and-seek mission, they were almost discovered, not by Bad Brogdon or Cutlass Curt, but by a monkey! On this day, Thomas and Barney had ventured further than they had ever gone before. Past two compartments and many containers, the excitement of doing something different continued to lure them deeper into the hull of the ship. As the crew entertained themselves above decks, Thomas didn't feel a concern to get back quickly, so they continued on. Although they had not discovered many new things, the change of scenery was welcome. Having ventured so far and been gone so long, Thomas thought maybe it was time to start heading back to their hiding place. Then it happened. As they turned around, both Thomas and Barney could not believe what they saw. It was not only just a monkey; it was Bad Brogdon's monkey. Thomas knew this was not good. The monkey was as surprised to see them as they were to see it. As though they had trespassed into its space, the monkey began to squeal and chatter as it jumped up and down. Thomas knew this would draw attention and Bad Brogdon would soon come down to check on all the commotion. Trying to get back quickly and undetected was hard enough, but even more so with a monkey following them. Back through the ship they hurried, Thomas, Barney, and the screaming monkey bringing up the rear. Drawing closer to their quarters, Thomas knew that if they didn't lose the monkey, they would soon be caught. Stopping to rest for moment, Thomas could hear a voice coming from a nearby ladder. It was none other than Bad Brogdon!

"José, José, what's all the commotion? Come here, my little friend."

Thomas thought, *well, this is it. Today we're caught.* Then suddenly, Barney, sensing the predicament, made a lunge at the monkey. The monkey, not wanting to tangle with Barney, turned and ran away, still screaming and jumping. When Thomas and Barney finally got back, Thomas thought how lucky they were that José the monkey could not talk. *Had he been able to, Barney would have eight lives left and I wouldn't have any.* "Thanks to you, Barney, we made it back safely," whispered Thomas.

Land and Ship Ahead

"Land ahead, Land ahead!" It was early morning on the fourteenth day, and Thomas was awakened by the call, "Land ahoy! Land ahoy!" He got up and could not believe what he was hearing. Could it be that they had already arrived at their destination? *No way*, thought Thomas. Thomas had heard conversations between the sailors, when they had discussed long voyages, which sometimes took months rather than weeks. He had also heard a conversation above decks the day before about being off the coast of Africa, and that was a long way from Tahiti and the Pitcairn Islands.

Thomas could plainly hear the sailor as he yelled from atop the crow's nest, "Land off the starboard bow!"

First Mate Douglas raised his spyglass and ordered one of the sailors to inform the captain that they were approaching the Canary Islands.

Thomas thought *would this be a good time to jump ship and try to get back home?* Then, after further consideration, Thomas knew that even if he and Barney were able to swim to an island, how would they get to another ship or the mainland? Although he and Barney would be off the HMS *Provider*, would they make it to land? Or possibly be captured by pirates? The risk was too great. Thomas raised the hatch cover to try and get a glimpse of the islands. As Thomas scanned the horizon, he could not see anything but water. "Let's see," he said, "starboard, okay, that would be on the right side. No wonder I don't see anything. I'm on the left side, which is the port side."

65

As the ship drew closer to the islands, Thomas could see land, but this land had white sandy beaches and strange kinds of trees. This was a lot different than the rocky coast of England. "I wonder if they really have canaries on these islands. I don't see anything but seagulls."

As Thomas scanned the horizon, he noticed something else. Thomas excitedly whispered to Barney, "Another ship is approaching." Thomas had to take a second look to make sure he was not seeing things. "Yes! It's another ship. I wonder if the crew sees it." Thomas wanted to yell but knew he couldn't. About that time, Thomas could hear the sailor in the crow's nest yell, "Ship is approaching aft, port side!"

Upon hearing this, Captain Flowers immediately raised his spyglass. "What do you make of her, Mr. Christian?" the captain inquired.

"Can't tell at this point, Captain, but let's hope she's a friendly one. Looks as though she is heading on our course," said the First Mate.

"Let's keep a close eye on her," said Captain Flowers.

"Aye, aye, Captain," replied First Mate Douglas.

As they drew near to the islands, Thomas could see that the other ship was getting closer. *This is going to get very interesting*, Thomas thought. There's a ship approaching from the rear with an island dead ahead and one on the right. This is going to get interesting and quickly.

"Captain, by the cut of her jib I'd say she's a sloop," said First Mate Douglas.

"Aye, Mr. Christian, and from whence she comes, I'd say she has a crew of Barbary corsairs aboard," said Captain Flowers. "Just in case, have the gunners load the forward swivel with a round shot and two eight-pounders with flying angels," said the captain.

"Aye, aye, Captain," replied First Mate Douglas.

The sailors aboard the *Provider* were now moving at double time preparing for a possible confrontation with a pirate ship. With Captain Flowers prior experiences at sea, he was not going to take anything for granted. He knew how ruthless Barbary corsairs could be. "If she thinks she's going to carry us, she'll have another thought coming."

As Captain Flowers raised his spyglass again to try and identify the ship, a gunner yelled, "Cannons ready, sir!"

"Captain, she's still holding course, but gaining," said First Mate Douglas.

"Aye, Mr. Douglas, she's definitely a sloop, and a fast one at that," said the captain.

Land and Ship Ahead

"I can make out two sailors, sir, but no flag," said the First Mate.

"Just as I thought, she'll be showing her true colors in due time." As the sloop came closer, Captain Flowers ordered his helmsman to hold course for the island straight ahead.

"Aye, aye, Captain."

No sooner was this said than First Mate Douglas yelled, "She's raised the Jolly Roger, Captain!"

Captain Flowers then ordered his crew to stand by. "We know her intentions now, so when she gets just within firing range, send a warning shot from the swivel across her bow," ordered Captain Flowers.

Although Thomas and Barney were tucked away below decks, Thomas could only imagine what might happen if a sea battle ensued, and just how safe he would be.

Close Call

"It's a pirate ship and ready to take us on. Captain, she's just about in firing range," said the First Mate.

Captain Flowers yelled, "Fire across her bow!"

Boom, echoed the cannon, as the shell crossed just forward of the bow and splashed into the sea. The pirate ship got the message and backed off slightly. However, because of her speed, the sloop was now approximately amidships.

"Captain, I believe the 'sea rats' got the message," said First Mate Douglas.

"Don't count on it, Mr. Douglas. If they did, it will only be because they think we have more cannons and men than they do," the captain explained.

It was almost as though the pirates had read his mind. The sloop suddenly made an almost ninety-degree turn and headed toward the *Provider*. The distance from the island straight ahead and the pirate ship on the port side were approximately the same. Both the pirate ship and the island were now drawing dangerously close

"Shall we prepare to fire another round, Captain?" First Mate Douglas asked.

"Hold your fire. Have the gunners train both eight-pounders on her forecastle and main mast, but do not fire until I give the command. Upon firing, I want a hard right rudder," commanded Captain Flowers.

"Did you say a hard right rudder, Captain?" asked Boatswain Christian.

"Indeed I did, Mr. Christian," said the captain.

"But, Captain, do you not see the island to our starboard and the one dead ahead?" asked First Mate Douglas.

"Mr. Douglas, I have sailed these waters before! Now stand by!" said the captain.

"Aye, aye, sir," snapped the First Mate.

The sloop and the island ahead were getting precariously close. Although Mr. Christian had not sailed here before, he knew how risky it was when sailing in shallow waters. The sloop was approaching at breakneck speed and appeared to be on a collision course with the port bow.

"Steady!" Captain Flowers yelled as the sloop moved within fifty yards. "Steady…steady…fire!"

Boom! Boom! Both cannons fired almost simultaneously. Even though below decks, Thomas and Barney could feel the concussion from these large cannons as the command "Hard right rudder!" rang out. As the ship rolled left, Thomas could almost touch the water, as well as the island that was in front of them. Then it came, a jarring, scraping sound that scared both Thomas and Barney.

Oh no! Have we run aground? Thomas wondered. Then came a crashing sound and yells from the pirate sloop. Although one shot missed, the other found its mark.

With one shot having ripped through its rigging, the sloop could not maintain the same sharp turn as the *Provider*. By waiting until the last minute to fire and come about, Captain Flowers drew the pirates into a deadly maneuver they could not recover from. With only one sail left, the pirate sloop slammed into the small island while trying desperately to make the same turn as the *Provider*. Thomas and Barney could hear the sailors above yelling with excitement as they celebrated the grounding of the pirate sloop.

"Mr. Douglas, go below decks and check for any leaks, and also take a sounding. If all is well, maintain our course through this cut and then set a south-southwest course," said the captain.

"Aye, aye, Captain," replied First Mate Douglas, who could not believe what he had just witnessed. Although he had plenty of sailing experience, he had never seen a captain command a ship through a situation like this. It only added to the respect that First Mate Douglas had for Captain Flowers.

After seeing a sailor walking below decks, Thomas could hear him yell, "No visible leaks, sir."

Close Call

At about that same time, another sailor could be heard saying, "Ten fathoms, sir."

"Very well," Captain Flowers replied. "Close-haul the sails and maintain our heading."

Crew Celebration

With the Canary Islands behind them, the crew was still celebrating its victory over the pirate ship. Captain Flowers decided to have a special supper that night for the crew to give thanks for a job well done. As the food was being prepared and the aroma drifted throughout the ship, Thomas could only hope that he would have a chance to sample some. The smell of the stew reminded Thomas of his mom's good cooking and how much he missed it.

Before the celebration supper began, First Mate Douglas gathered the crew together on the main deck so that Captain Flowers could address the men. He began by thanking the crew for a job well done. During the discussion of that day's encounter, one of the crew members expressed a concern that they had almost had the same dismal ending as the pirate ship. That comment was made by none other than Bad Brogdon. Upon hearing the comment, Captain Flowers stepped forward and asked who had made that questionable remark.

"I did, Captain, but no harm was intended," was the response.

Taking a more defensive stand, Captain Flowers snapped back, "Are you questioning my ability to captain this ship?"

Everyone got really quiet as Brogdon responded sharply, "No, sir."

"Very well," Captain Flowers said with authority. "And by the way, that was not only a great job each of you did, but I also planned that little brush with the bottom." Captain Flowers said with a slight smile, "You see, it was about time for a good ship careening."

Upon hearing that, the crew exploded with jubilant laughter and applause. Captain Flowers continued, "Before beginning this voyage, I had hoped that we would not encounter a situation like we did today. However, we did, and I am very proud of the way each of you responded. I wish I could promise you that we will not have another experience like this again, but I can't. However, if we do, I'm convinced that each of you will respond in the same professional manner. Now, let's have a little celebration. I have instructed Mr. Christian to dole out an extra ration of beer to go along with our special supper. Enjoy yourselves, men, job well done."

As the evening progressed, Thomas and Barney could hear the crew laughing, singing, and having a good time. Thomas thought how much fun it would be if he could be there. Now he could only hope that he and Barney would be able to sample the special meal later that night.

Celebration Below Decks

The lanterns were lit and the crew was still enjoying the celebration. With all hands above decks, and getting very hungry, Thomas decided to make his nightly move to forage for food. Although some of the food, like the hardtack and dried beef, was nearby, the special stew for the celebration supper had been prepared in the galley. Thomas knew that it would take some careful maneuvering between the spaces not to get caught or detected. Sometimes crouching and other times crawling, Thomas and Barney made their way to the cooking area, where the big iron pot sat simmering on the hot coals under it. It was like a pot at the end of a rainbow, except with food, not gold, Thomas thought, as he looked around to make sure no one was about.

"Okay, the coast is clear, Barney. Let's make our move." With only the makeshift wooden bowl and spoon he had carved earlier, Thomas hurried over to the pot and looked in. Thank goodness there was some left! Knowing that Barney was just as hungry, Thomas put a little on the floor and Barney began lapping it up. Although it was not his mother's and he didn't know what was in it, Thomas enjoyed every morsel. "Okay, Barney, time's up. I'll fill the bowl and take it back with us."

No sooner had Thomas filled his bowl and turned to leave than footsteps were heard coming down the ladder. "Hurry, Barney, get behind the barrel," whispered Thomas.

As Thomas peeked around the barrel, he could see two sailors walking toward the pot. As they drew closer, even in the dim light Thomas could make out who they were. No surprise; it was Bad Brogdon and Cutlass Curt. Thomas was so close he could smell them. Yes, it was that same smell he remembered from in front of Pelican Pete's Pub. Not knowing whether or not they had permission to get additional food, Thomas could only imagine that they were stealing, as they had done before. It was confirmed when he overheard Cutlass Curt say in a low voice, "Those sprogs we have on board will never miss our little additional taste of stew and beer."

"I'll drink to that, Mr. Curt. If anyone deserves it, the captain and his first mate do," Brogdon said in a raspy voice, as he grinned and raised his cup to drink. "However, we'll need to shake a leg, Mr. Curt, before we're caught and reduced in rank."

"Aye, aye, Captain," Cutlass Curt said, as if to resign himself to the fact that he was now under Bad Brogdon's command.

The Doldrums

Three weeks at sea and nothing had changed except the weather. The temperature had risen substantially and it was starting to get downright hot below decks. Thomas knew from his studies at school that the ship had probably entered the Doldrums—areas near the equator where the trade winds ceased to blow or blew very slightly. Although all sails were up, it seemed that the huge ship was barely moving. Thomas thought back on how rough and cold the North Atlantic had been. Now it appeared he had the opposite, no wind and hot temperatures. But this meant one good thing, if one could call it that: no seasickness. Barney had adjusted well to the heat and was not doing as much roaming as he had been. Even several passing mice could not arouse him enough to make the hunt. If there was anything else good to say about calm seas, it was that Thomas could carve away without the fear of cutting his fingers, and carve he did. For the next three days, Thomas continued to carve during the day and scavenge at night. However, carving this cat was somewhat difficult for Thomas, because the more he carved, the more he thought about his Memaw's special Barney High Tail cat he had sold to Bad Brogdon. As painful as it was, Thomas felt the drive to finish this carving. *Maybe if we ever get back home, it will be a special gift for my mom,* Thomas thought, as tears rolled down his face.

Painstakingly, Thomas was able to finish the special cat for his mom and was very proud of the work he had done. Except for the missing tiger eyes, the completed cat was almost identical to his original. *All I need now is some tiger eyes*, thought Thomas, as he held back more tears.

Hot Air Above and Below Decks

Five weeks had passed, and the southern trade winds started to pick up. Thomas thought that the type of hot air above decks was much better than the hot air below decks—meaning the conversations he was hearing between the two ruffians, Cutlass Curt and Bad Brogdon. Nothing they said was good. This made Thomas continue to wonder about their past. Complaints about the food rations, other sailors, and even the way the captain was commanding the ship were constantly heard. These negative conversations were bad, but the continual stealing of food and drink from the ship's storage was worse. *If only the captain knew,* Thomas thought. *Maybe another crew member will find out and tell him.*

Curiosity Almost Killed the Cat

Six weeks had passed, and the ship was well below the equator and out of the Doldrums. Being a little on the warm side, it was refreshing to have a sea breeze blowing through the hatch cover both day and night. It appeared that the crew also enjoyed getting out of the stagnant seas. Although below decks, Thomas had already learned several things about sailors. One was that if land was not in sight, the next best thing was a full wind at your back. Thomas had noticed a direct correlation between full sails and higher spirits.

One late afternoon, Thomas and Barney heard a scraping sound coming from one of the nearby crates. Not knowing if it was the two ruffian sailors breaking into one of the food barrels, Thomas was at first reluctant to try and identify the source of the sound. However, as the sound continued and increased, he could no longer stand it. *I've just got to find out what's going on,* Thomas thought. *If those two ruffians are stealing food again, they sure are taking their time.*

Crawling between and around the crates, Thomas and Barney were now extremely close. *Just beyond this one last barrel,* Thomas thought, as he crawled one way and Barney the other. As Thomas peeked around the barrel, he was shocked to discover that he was face-to-face with none other than José the

81

monkey! That's right, Bad Brogdon's big brown monkey, which had a long tail just like Barney's.

As soon as Thomas was spotted, the monkey did a back flip and landed directly on top of Barney, who was approaching from the opposite direction. This touched off complete pandemonium, with Barney and the monkey racing around the crates and barrels at breakneck speed. Thomas could not believe Barney could run that fast, but with a monkey on one's back, anyone could. The screaming monkey finally jumped off and leaped from one barrel to the next, heading straight up the ladder to the main deck. Except for some minor scratches, Barney made it through the ordeal and was glad to get back to Thomas. However, because of all the noise that monkey had made, several sailors came to look around the compartment.

Thomas whispered, "Quiet, Barney, don't move." *If I could just get my hands on that monkey*, Thomas thought, as the sailors turned and headed back up to the main deck.

Glimmer of Hope

Seven weeks had passed, and the prevailing westerly winds were pushing the ship at a steady pace. Thomas had heard that if the winds continued, they would be rounding Cape Horn within a week or so. This was welcome news because it meant they were now well over halfway to their destination. If Captain Gates and the *Venture* could be located quickly, they could be returning home soon—that is, if everything went as expected, and Thomas and Barney remained undetected. *That's a lot of ifs*, Thomas thought.

As Thomas sat looking at the days and weeks he had notched in the wood, the word "undetected" crossed his mind again. He was running out of room on the bulkhead to notch any more days. *If I continue, the chance of someone seeing it increases*, thought Thomas. *I have to figure out another way of tracking time. I've got it!* Thomas knew that each notch represented a day and each cross represented Sunday and the end of that week. *I'll just go back and add a horizontal line to each notch for the additional days. This will keep the carved area on the bulkhead to a minimum and lessen the chance that someone will see it.* The resolution of tracking time and thinking about home allowed Thomas to have a peaceful sleep.

Discovered

After a good night's sleep, Thomas and Barney were up and at 'em. "Well, Barney, I'm feeling pretty good this morning. Why don't we try and find something special to eat today?" said Thomas, as he gazed at all the barrels and crates. Thomas knew that most of the original fresh foods were gone or spoiled. No more sweet bread, vegetables, or fruit. The hardtack had weevils but was still edible. The water had become a little tainted but was still drinkable. "Barney, let's go see what we can uncover," said Thomas. So off they went, foraging from one barrel and crate to another. "Look, Barney, dried dates! What a surprise! I wonder how these would taste with smoked beef?" said Thomas. "I know, Barney, you would prefer the dried fish. Okay, let's have both, along with some pickled eggs."

After Thomas had filled all his pockets with dried beef and fish, he quickly filled his little wooden bowl with some pickled cackle fruit (eggs). "Time to go home now, Barney," said Thomas. No sooner had Thomas uttered these words than he realized what he had just said. "No, this is not my home! I miss my home, my real home!"

As Thomas turned to start back, the sound of steps could be heard coming from the nearby ladder. "Hurry, Barney, let's get back quickly," said Thomas. Not realizing how full his pockets were, Thomas left a trail of food all the way back to their hiding place. In addition to that, Barney had stopped several barrels away and was eating a piece of the dried fish that had been dropped. Thomas could hear the footsteps and voices getting closer.

"It's either that bloody monkey or a big rat," said one of the sailors.

"In either case, we will soon find out. Look, the little devil has left us a trail," said a different voice.

Thomas suddenly realized what had happened, and he felt of the remaining food in his pockets. *Maybe Barney will finish that last scrap and get back here before the sailors get closer.*

Thomas sat motionless behind the last barrel as the two sailors quietly tiptoed very close to where Barney sat eating his fish. Thomas could not say a word, but tried to get Barney's attention by waving for the cat to come to him. Barney was either too hungry or he could not see Thomas. Either way, it was not good. Although Barney was out of sight, one thing was slightly visible between two barrels: the tip of Barney's tail!

As the two sailors crept closer, one whispered to the other, "Look, there's that little rat! I'll crush him against the bulkhead!" Then suddenly, one of the sailor's shoes came crashing down on Barney's tail. Pandemonium ensued. Barney let out with a hair-raising scream as he appeared to be shot straight from a cannon. Thomas heard one of the sailors say, "I got him,"

Thomas immediately jumped up and shouted, "Stop that! Barney, are you okay?"

"Well, look what we've discovered. Not one but two rats!" said the sailor.

"That's my cat! Don't you hurt him!" said Thomas.

"Now, let's see, we have just discovered a thieving stowaway and his little friend, and we are to be kind?" asked the sailor.

"I'm not a thief, and neither is Barney," Thomas snapped back.

"Well, let's just see what the captain will say about this," said the sailor. Thomas was then grabbed by one of the sailors and led away while Barney ran for his life.

Facing the Captain

Thomas always knew it could happen, but had hoped beyond hope it wouldn't. As he was being led up and onto the main deck, the sailors looked on with amazement. Then, the snide comments started.

"I see ye discovered a rat, matey."

"He's a bit wee for a stowaway."

With head bowed and scared to death, Thomas could only look down and wonder what his fate would be.

As they walked to the captain's quarters, they were stopped by First Mate Douglas. "Well, what do we have here, sailors?" asked Mr. Douglas.

"Well, sir, we caught the little thieving stowaway and his cat in the storage area below decks," answered Brogdon.

"Stowaway, eh? What's your name, lad?" asked First Mate Douglas.

"Thomas Pilgrim, sir, and my cat is Barney High Tail," answered Thomas.

"What are you doing aboard our ship, Thomas Pilgrim?" asked the first mate.

"Well, sir, it's a long story," said Thomas.

"Then why don't you wait and tell it to the captain," said Mr. Douglas.

Thomas's heart raced as they stood before the captain's door. After several knocks and Mr. Douglas identifying himself, Captain Flowers responded, "Come in."

As Thomas and Barney stood close behind Mr. Douglas, the door was opened slightly.

Mr. Douglas said, "Captain, we have discovered a stowaway aboard our ship."

"Stowaway," responded Captain Flowers.

"Yes, sir, and I have him here," said Mr. Douglas.

"Bring him in, Mr. Douglas," said the captain.

As the door opened slowly, Thomas felt his heart pounding and he could hardly walk.

"Get in there, lad!" Mr. Douglas said, as he steered Thomas around by his arm.

"Well, what do we have here?" Captain Flowers asked, as he looked up from his desk. Thomas was so scared he could not speak. "What's the matter, lad? Cat got your tongue?"

Immediately, Thomas thought about Barney. *I hope Barney is okay.*

"What are you doing aboard our ship, lad?" asked Captain Flowers.

"Well, sir, it was an accident," answered Thomas.

"An accident?" asked the captain.

"Yes sir. You see, we only wanted to visit the ship," said Thomas.

"Wait a minute, I think I recognize you. Your dad helped build our ship, and you're the lad that did the carvings at the dock," said the captain.

"Yes, sir, that's me!" said Thomas.

"I also remember you gave some of your earnings to help our voyage. Well, lad, tell me how you ended up being a stowaway," said the captain.

"Well, sir, as I said, it was an accident. My friend Christopher and I only wanted to spend the night on the ship before it sailed, and we were caught. Christopher got off and I got hurt," explained Thomas.

"Hurt?" asked the captain.

"Yes, sir, I sprained my foot and couldn't walk. I wanted to, but I couldn't. My plan was to leave the ship before morning, but I fell asleep and woke up when the ship was leaving. It was too late, and we had to stay aboard," said Thomas.

"What do you mean, *we*? I thought you said your friend got off?" asked the captain.

"Yes, sir, my friend Christopher did, but Barney High Tail, my cat, stayed with me," said Thomas.

"A cat, eh! No wonder we haven't seen many rats on board," said the captain. Thomas didn't know whether to smile or not. "Well, lad, do you have any idea what is normally done with stowaways that are discovered aboard ships?"

"No, sir, I don't," replied Thomas.

"We will let you know in due time. Now, let's find your cat and see if both of you could use some food," said the captain.

"Thank you, sir," replied Thomas.

"Captain, where shall we keep the lad?" asked the First Mate.

"While I decide, he will remain confined to my quarters," answered Captain Flowers. "With that said, Mr. Douglas, why don't you escort the lad below decks to locate his cat, and return both to me."

"Aye, aye, sir," said Mr. Douglas.

When Mr. Douglas and Thomas headed back across the main deck, Cutlass Curt and Bad Brogdon could be heard talking with some of the other sailors and pointing to Thomas. As they passed, Bad Brogdon said, "That's the little thieving stowaway we caught."

One of the other sailors responded, "Maybe the captain will maroon him."

"Or even better, hang him," said another sailor.

Upon hearing that, Mr. Douglas turned and gave the sailors a scathing look, and then continued walking down the ladder and below decks. Thomas led the way back through and around the crates and barrels. "Here we are," Thomas said, as he looked around for Barney.

"So this is where you've been living, eh, lad?" asked Mr. Douglas.

"Yes, sir," Thomas replied.

"And this must be where you marked off the days at sea?" asked First Mate Douglas.

"Yes sir. And here is my cat, Barney High Tail," said Thomas.

Although Barney could hear Thomas's voice, he was still reluctant to get close to Mr. Douglas.

"Its okay, Barney," Thomas said, as he coaxed Barney out into the open. He reached down and picked up the cat. "It's okay, Barney, we have a new home for now."

Back to the captain's quarters they went, with Thomas clutching Barney like a baby. As they entered, Thomas wondered what would happen next. Captain Flowers was now sitting at a small table next to his desk.

"So this is your companion Barney, the cat?" asked the captain.

"Yes, sir, but his real name is Barney High Tail," said Thomas.

"Barney High Tail?" said the captain.

"Yes sir. His tail was actually higher, but it got broken," said Thomas.

"Got broken?" asked the captain.

"Yes, sir, one of the sailors thought his tail was a rat's and hit it," said Thomas.

Captain Flowers chuckled and said, "I know it's not funny, lad, but your cat, Barney, does look like he's moving even though he's standing still."

Thomas smiled slightly in agreement.

"Son, why don't you set the cat down and join me for supper? I want to hear more about how you've managed to live aboard our ship," said Captain Flowers.

As Thomas sat before the captain, he could not believe that he was actually going to eat off a plate with his own knife, fork, and spoon. Also, to his surprise, he was being served by one of the crew members.

"Are you hungry, lad?" asked Captain Flowers.

"Yes, sir," replied Thomas, as he gazed down at his plate.

"Don't be bashful, lad, you can eat as much as you want," said the captain.

"Thank you, sir. But would you mind if I gave thanks?" asked Thomas.

"Not at all, please go ahead," replied the captain.

As Thomas began to pray, the emotions of the day and his longing for his family became apparent, and he began to weep.

Captain Flowers sensed Thomas's feelings, and he moved around the table and sat next to Thomas. He put his arm around Thomas and said, "I understand, lad. Maybe you will feel better after a good meal."

"Thank you, sir. Would it be okay if I gave Barney some scraps?" asked Thomas.

"Certainly lad, we'll even give him his own plate," said the captain.

"Oh, thank you, sir," Thomas replied.

That evening, Thomas felt somewhat less stressed as he shared his encounter with Captain Flowers.

Several hours passed, and Captain Flowers sensed that Thomas was getting tired. "It's been a busy day, lad, why don't we call it a day?" said Captain Flowers. Thomas yawned and wondered where he would sleep. "Now that you've been discovered, lad, I think it's best that you stay here. I've prepared a place for you to sleep. Oh, and your cat, Barney Bent Tail, can stay as well."

Thomas smiled and said, "Thank you, sir."

Even though Captain Flowers snored like the wind in the sails, it was the best night's sleep Thomas had had since he began the voyage.

Facing the Crew

Several days had passed, and Thomas and Barney had not ventured out of the captain's quarters for fear of retribution from the crew. However, like the seas, conversations about Thomas were beginning to rise. Captain Flowers had decided to address the situation with the crew and had called all of them to the main deck. Thomas accompanied Captain Flowers while Barney stayed behind.

"Good morning, men. I've called you together this morning to discuss a situation which I'm sure most of you are aware of. Several days ago, this lad and his cat were discovered hiding aboard our ship. After hearing his unfortunate story, I've decided to keep him aboard until a way is found to return him home."

Bad Brogdon immediately spoke up and said, "Captain, should he not be punished?"

Thomas looked intently at Brogdon as the conversation continued.

"Under normal circumstances, I would suggest severe punishment, but not in this case," said the captain.

"Not to disagree with you, Captain, but catching a thief aboard our ship does not require severe punishment? If the lad does not dance the hempen jig (be hung), I would suggest he receive the cat-o'-nine-tails (be whipped)," suggested Brogdon.

"I'll make the decision on his punishment, Mr. Brogdon. But let's have the lad speak," said the captain.

As the crew stared at Thomas, he began speaking in a soft voice. "Sir, I know that I have taken some rations and some punishment is deserved. If its okay, I'll learn to dance the hempen jig before the crew, rather than have another cat, especially one with nine tails," said Thomas.

When the crew heard this, loud laughter broke out. Thomas could not understand why.

"Belay the laughter," Captain Flowers said. "There'll be neither. You see, while this lad was visiting our ship he was, unfortunately, injured and could not get off."

Thomas realized that Captain Flowers was really trying to help him by not reinforcing the fact that he and Christopher had snuck on board in the first place.

Bad Brogdon bore in again by saying, "His story is believable, but his actions make him a thief."

Thomas could no longer take the accusations, and blurted out, "I'm not a thief. We had to eat, and if anybody is a thief, it's you and your friend, Mr. Curt."

"That's strong language, lad," said Captain Flowers.

"Yes, sir, but I saw them with my own eyes," said Thomas.

"Not true, Captain, the lad is just trying to pass the blame," said Brogdon.

At that time, First Mate Douglas sensed where the conversation was headed and tried to diffuse the situation. "Captain, may I suggest a fair restitution for the food that the lad, shall I say, *borrowed*?"

"What might that be, Mr. Douglas?"

"In addition to being your cabin boy, he would be a deck swab until such time as he leaves our ship," said First Mate Douglas.

"Mr. Douglas, I believe this to be a fair and equitable resolution, and may I add that he will remain under my command until such time. Are there any questions from our crew?" asked Captain Flowers.

No one spoke, but both Bad Brogdon and Cutlass Curt stared intently at Thomas as he headed back toward the captain's quarters behind Captain Flowers.

Upon entering his quarters, Captain Flowers summoned Mr. Douglas. When First Mate Douglas entered, Captain Flowers sat down and said to Thomas, "Now, let's hear the whole story about certain sailors stealing food aboard this ship." After Thomas told the whole story to Captain Flowers and First Mate Douglas, Captain Flowers said that he would take everything under consideration, and dismissed Mr. Douglas.

Rounding the Horn

Over eight weeks had passed, and the HMS *Provider* was rounding Cape Horn on the southernmost tip of South America. The wind and seas had picked up substantially. Because of the lurching ship, Thomas and Barney had been restricted to the captain's quarters. Thomas thought for a while that he had earned his sea legs, but not quite. The heavy seas were as bad as or worse than what he had experienced in the North Atlantic. Even Captain Flowers did not venture out of his quarters except to speak to First Mate Douglas. The only good things were that the wind and seas were coming from the southwest, which meant the captain could continue to hold a close course to the final destination, the Pitcairn Islands. However, holding the huge ship on course became more difficult as the swells increased in size. As soon as the ship crested one wave and started down, another was there to wash over the bow. Higher and higher the waves grew. The bow would disappear when the ship came crashing down. Thomas, more frightened than seasick, held on for dear life. Even Captain Flowers looked somewhat concerned as he tried to keep from falling.

Sensing Thomas's condition, Captain Flowers slid a bucket over to him, saying, "Use it if you need it."

Upon hearing that, Thomas leaned over and let it fly. Grasping the bucket with one hand and holding on to the bulkhead with the other, Thomas could only sit and wait on the next round of nausea. *Oh, will it ever stop?* Thomas wondered, as his dry heaves continued.

Just as he was thinking it could not get any worse, a sudden loud crack was heard. The foremast came crashing down, taking out part of the mainmast and sails. As the mast landed on the deck, several crew members were hit by falling debris. One was killed instantly and the other was pinned beneath the heavy mast. Without the sails, the ship took a hard roll starboard, and the crew fought to free the crewmen and hold the ship on course. Howling winds, crashing waves, and the sound of cargo breaking loose could be heard below decks. It was taking two crewmen to hold and turn the helm. Before the ship could adjust its course, a huge wave passed over the larboard side, washing one sailor overboard. His cries for help could barely be heard as the ship continued being tossed about. Thomas could only pray that the ship remained afloat and the seas would soon calm.

Hours passed, and suddenly the wind and seas subsided. The crew continued to make repairs as Captain Flowers assessed the damage. One crewman dead, one assumed dead, one severely injured, and many more with cuts and bruises.

The next morning, Captain Flowers mustered the crew as repairs continued. It was a sad and solemn day as they laid to rest the dead crewman. Captain Flowers knew it would be a futile attempt to try and locate one missing crewman. However, he openly prayed that the sailor had died peacefully, and he thanked the crew for a courageous job in keeping the ship afloat. A splint was applied to the crewman's broken leg by the surgeon and attention was given to the other injured crewmen. With sails patched and rigging repaired, the HMS *Provider* pressed on.

Cabin Boy and Powder Monkey

With calmer seas and most repairs made, the HMS *Provider* was back on course. Thomas had assumed his new position as cabin boy. Keeping the captain's quarters clean, helping the cook, and swabbing the decks were everyday tasks. Barney appeared to have it made, curled up and sleeping most of the day on top of the captain's desk. Although Thomas had daily chores, he welcomed the freedom of moving about the ship without the fear of getting caught. The only disturbing things were the ugly comments and glares given by Bad Brogdon and Cutlass Curt. It got so bad that Thomas was afraid to leave the captain's quarters.

One evening, Thomas could no longer hold back and told Captain Flowers how he was being treated. Captain Flowers listened intently. When Thomas finished talking, Captain Flowers said, "Thomas, tell me again about the incident."

"Which incident sir?" Thomas replied.

"Oh, was there more than one?" asked the captain.

"Yes sir. There were a number of times I observed them below decks," said Thomas.

"Tell me again exactly what they were doing each time," said the captain.

"Sir, they were stealing food and drink," answered Thomas.

"How about the conversations? Could you hear anything they were saying?" asked the captain.

"It was hard at times because they always whispered, but one time I heard them saying something about being the captain and first mate of this ship," said Thomas.

"That's enough, lad. Now, I would like for you to go and assist our cook with this evening's meal. On your way, ask Mr. Douglas to come to my quarters immediately," said Captain Flowers.

"Yes, sir, Captain," Thomas replied as he left.

That evening, while Thomas was helping the cook hand out the plates of food, another incident happened that really bothered him. As Thomas was getting ready to set a plate down on the table, Cutlass Curt turned and grabbed it from Thomas. He placed his hand over Thomas's and pressed it tightly against the metal plate. As he increased the pressure on Thomas's hand, Thomas noticed an evil glare that he had never seen before from Cutlass Curt. The pressure was so great that Thomas thought his hand was going to break. Thomas did not mention this incident to Captain Flowers for fear of what Curt might do.

Ghost Ship

The next day, as the ship sailed through calm waters, the lookout in the crow's nest yelled, "Ship, dead ahead!"

Being concerned about pirates, especially after their first encounter, First Mate Douglas lifted his spyglass to scan the horizon. Not only was there another ship, but several small islands just beyond it. With islands nearby, this could mean shallow water. Captain Flowers ordered Mr. Douglas to take a depth sounding before getting any closer.

"Eight fathoms, sir," said Mr. Douglas.

"Very well, let's keep a sharp eye on the depth," ordered Captain Flowers.

"Aye, aye, sir," Mr. Douglas replied.

After several minutes, the crewman yelled to Mr. Douglas, "Sir, it appears the ship is dead in the water."

"Dead in the water?" asked Mr. Douglas.

"Yes, sir, I see no sails," replied the crewman.

Mr. Douglas thought, *this could mean several things. They could have sailed around the Horn and experienced some damage to their sails and other rigging, or something worse, or it could be a pirate decoy.*

As they sailed closer, Captain Flowers was taking no chances. "Mr. Douglas, have the gunners load two eight-pounders and a saker larboard side. Also, let me know what flag they are flying. We will make a wide circle to try and identify the ship." *Could it possibly be the* Venture? Captain Flowers wondered.

When the *Provider* was within several hundred yards, Captain Flowers said, "No sails, no flag, and, it appears, no crew. Something's amiss. Take her in closer, Mr. Douglas, and have the gunners on standby. If it's a decoy, we will be ready."

"Aye, aye, sir," said Douglas.

Now within one hundred yards, it appeared that the ship was devoid of any crew, but Captain Flowers was still not taking any chances. "Take in all sails and lower the cockboat. I want several armed crewmen to board and inspect this ship before we pull alongside," he said.

"Aye, aye, sir," Boatswain Christian said. "I'll have our boarding party do a thorough investigation of the ship."

The small boat was lowered and the two sailors paddled toward the ship. As they climbed aboard and onto the main deck, an eerie feeling came over them.

"Ahoy! Ahoy there! Anybody aboard?" yelled one of the sailors. There was total silence.

"This is like a ghost ship," said the other sailor.

"You're right, it's kind of spooky," said the first. Except for the missing crew, sails, and cannons, the ship was pretty much intact. "Let's have a look below decks."

With lanterns lit, the two sailors started down the hatchway ladder. A strong, rank odor came drifting up from below decks, and the two sailors could not believe what they saw.

"This is not a ghost ship, it's a slave ship," said one.

Right before their eyes lay three dead slaves. No one else was found aboard the ship. When the sailors returned to the *Provider*, they reported to the captain what they had found.

"Captain, it looks as though this was a slave ship that was plundered by pirates. We found no one except three dead slaves," said one of the sailors.

"What shape is the ship in?" asked the captain.

"The ship looks sound, Captain. Not much water in the bilge, and the bulkheads look good," said the other sailor.

"Let's take a closer look," said Captain Flowers.

The captain ordered the HMS *Provider* to pull alongside the slave ship so that he could board it. After the two ships were secured, Captain Flowers ordered that the dead slaves be brought to the main deck for a proper burial. When the three slaves were brought up from below decks and laid next to each other, Captain Flowers noticed the distinctive skin color and strange tattoos on one of the slaves. Intrigued by the tattoos, Captain Flowers wanted the corpse to be rolled over. As the crewman grabbed the slave's torso to roll him over, he immediately stopped and said, "Sir, this slave is still warm and appears to be breathing!"

"Are you sure?" asked the captain.

"Yes, sir, I can see his chest and eyes moving," answered the crewman.

"Get this man on our ship and out of the sun! Also, have the surgeon tend to him immediately."

"Aye, Captain," Mr. Christian responded.

The slave was carefully moved to the HMS *Provider*. "Where shall we put him, Captain?"

"Put him in my quarters for the time being. If he makes it, we'll move him to the crew's quarters," answered the captain.

"Aye, aye, sir."

Captain Flowers continued his inspection of the ship, along with the first mate. "Mr. Douglas, I've been thinking for the last couple of days about Captain Gates and the crew of the *Venture*. What if they have had the misfortune of being marooned on one of the surrounding islands? My concern then would be, how would we get them back home if they are located?"

"That's a good point, Captain. But what if we had this ship along with ours? We could certainly do it then, but the ship would have to be outfitted," said Mr. Douglas.

"Do we have enough extra sails to get her under way?" asked Captain Flowers.

"Aye, sir. We probably have enough to get her under way, but having sufficient crew to sail her is the question," said Mr. Douglas. "Captain, may I suggest that Mr. Christian take command of the slave ship? I will be happy to assume his duties for the time being."

"Very well Mr. Douglas. Let's get started on getting this ship seaworthy. I want only enough men to sail her, and would like to discuss with Mr. Christian about taking command of the new ship. Let me know as soon as she is ready to get under way."

Upon hearing that, Mr. Douglas ordered the crew to "turn to and look lively" in getting the ship ready.

Back aboard the *Provider*, while the slave was being attended to by the surgeon, Thomas sat watching intently. Several hours had gone by, and the surgeon continued to squeeze water onto the face and mouth of the almost dead slave. His eyes were still twitching and his mouth was now open. The surgeon looked at Thomas and said, "Lad, would you like to assist me in trying to bring this body back to life?"

"I'll be glad to help in any way I can," Thomas replied.

"Okay, you will need to continue to try and get as much water as possible into his mouth. If he lives, you will have done a good deed," said the surgeon. Thinking that it would only be a matter of time before the young slave died, the surgeon left him in Thomas's care.

All that afternoon and into the night, Thomas stayed with the young slave. If he died, it would not be because Thomas was not doing what he could do to keep him alive. The next morning, Thomas noticed more movement of the young slave's mouth. By tilting his head back, Thomas was able to pour a little more water into his mouth. All of a sudden, the young slave started coughing and opened his eyes. He glared strangely at Thomas, but he was not out of the woods yet. Weak and dehydrated, it would be several days before the young slave could take anything but water. Finally, the slave was able to move, and he even tried to speak. "Bobba Lucca, Bobba Lucca," he would repeat, time after time. Since no other understandable words were spoken, Captain Flowers had begun referring to him as Bobba Lucca.

Bobba Is Better

"How's Bobba Lucca doing this morning?" Captain Flowers asked, as he watched Thomas and the slave share a meal.

"He's doing a lot better, Captain," answered Thomas.

"Good. I think it might be time to move him to the crew's quarters," said the captain.

Not knowing how the crew, especially Bad Brogdon and Cutlass Curt, would treat him, Thomas asked the captain if Bobba Lucca could continue to stay in his quarters for a few more days. Thomas was hoping that the captain would by then have a soft spot in his heart for Thomas's new friend. After some consideration, Captain Flowers agreed to let Bobba Lucca stay in his cabin for a few days longer, with the understanding that he would have to work, just like the other crew members.

Another week passed and Bobba Lucca regained most of his strength. During a morning briefing, Captain Flowers told the crew that the young slave would become a member of the crew, and that he would work as a powder monkey and do any other tasks the captain gave him. A powder monkey's job included loading and keeping all guns cleaned. Since he had never done this before, he would be trained by one of the master gunners. Although Bobba Lucca could not speak English, he learned quickly by example. No one could have imagined how soon his newfound skill would be needed, but it turned out to be sooner rather than later.

HMS *Blackbird*

As the two ships lay anchored, the outfitting of the slave ship was just about finished. Captain Flowers called the crew together and decided that, since the new ship had carried slaves from Africa and islands in the South Pacific, he would name her the HMS *Blackbird*. Since they would need a crew to sail her, Captain Flowers first asked for volunteers. He explained that anyone that volunteered would sail with a limited crew, which would mean additional work, but, for giving up some of the conveniences aboard the HMS *Provider*, he agreed to increase their pay and give additional shore leave when they reached Tahiti. With that said, Captain Flowers asked for a show of hands from anyone interested in sailing the *Blackbird*. A number of crew members raised their hands, including Bad Brogdon and Cutlass Curt. Boatswain Christian agreed to command the ship while it was under way.

After a few minutes of discussion between Mr. Christian and the new crew members, Captain Flowers announced that, since the ships would be sailing the next day, he would like to have a special celebration that night for the crew. As the evening progressed, Brogdon and Curt could be heard talking about swimming ashore for the night, in hopes of finding friendship with the local islanders. They were quickly reminded by several other sailors of the shark-infested waters they were in. Even a night on Pitcairn Island would not be worth the risk.

Pirate Attack

Morning came, and Captain Flowers briefed the new crew of the HMS *Blackbird*. He ordered Mr. Christian to stay as close to the HMS *Provider* as possible. With a salute to Captain Flowers, Mr. Christian ordered his crew to set sail behind the *Provider*.

No sooner had the two ships gotten under way than another ship suddenly appeared off the north side of the island. Sailing behind the *Provider* and *Blackbird*, it looked as though the other ship was starting to follow them. The three ships looked like an English armada. Every move they made, the other ship responded. This went on for several hours before things changed. As if to check out the *Blackbird*, the mystery ship pulled alongside so close that its crew could be seen. Not having a full complement of sails, it would be impossible for the *Provider* and *Blackbird* to try and outrun the mystery ship. Sensing possible danger, Captain Flowers slowed the *Provider* to allow the *Blackbird* to draw as close as possible.

Then it happened: the mystery ship hoisted its colors. This was not good. The dreaded Jolly Roger was flying. Like a lion selecting its prey, the pirates chose the *Blackbird*. Without cannons, the pirates would have easy pickings of what might be on board. Considering their mission and all that was at stake, Captain Flowers would not go down without a fight. He ordered all cannons be loaded and put on standby. Several minutes passed as the pirate crew waited to see if the *Blackbird* would lower its sails. The pirates were now amidships and trained their cannons on the *Blackbird*. Boom!

A cannon blast across the bow had the *Blackbird* in a very dangerous situation. With no way to defend the ship or outrun them, Mr. Christian could only hope that Captain Flowers would see their peril and help. Seeing and hearing what had just happened, Captain Flowers ordered a hard left rudder and swung the *Provider* around one hundred and eighty degrees. While the ship was maneuvering, Captain Flowers ordered all hands to battle stations.

The *Provider* was now heading toward both ships. This would place the *Blackbird* on the starboard side and the approaching pirate ship on the larboard side. If all went well, the *Provider* would pass between the two ships, creating a shield for the *Blackbird* and giving it a chance to get out of cannon range.

One hundred yards and closing fast. Thomas was scared to death and had taken refuge in the captain's quarters, while Bobba Lucca was busy carrying gunpowder and various-sized cannonballs. Captain Flowers gave the command to stand by. Not taking any chances, he ordered the larger eight-pound cannons to fire first, followed by the smaller cannons when the pirate ship got within range.

Boom! Boom! Boom! Cannons on both ships fired almost simultaneously, and cannonballs ripped through the rigging and bulkheads of both ships. The sound was deafening, and Thomas crouched against the bulkhead with his eyes shut and his hands covering his ears. Having no cannons or a way to assist, the *Blackbird* could only stay a safe distance away as the battle ensued. Suddenly, a cannon blast struck the *Provider* within inches of Thomas's head! Splintering wood and smoke filled the room, as Thomas crawled under the captain's desk while searching for Barney. Blast after blast, the battle continued, and Thomas felt the impact of cannonballs striking the ship and heard the screams of injured crewmen.

Cut and bruised by the flying wood, Thomas laid crying and praying that the battle would soon end. Glancing through the captain's swinging door, Thomas could not believe the carnage before his eyes! Sails, rigging, guns, and the bodies of crewmen lay scattered across the deck. Screams for help and the smell of death made Thomas nauseous as he gazed out, looking for Captain Flowers and his friend, Bobba Lucca. Screams could also be heard coming from the burning pirate ship. The *Provider*, although not on fire, was starting to list badly. This could mean only one thing. It could be sinking.

Pirate Attack

Captain Flowers had been severely wounded and was taken to his quarters by First Mate Douglas and several other sailors. Because of the severity of his wounds, he ordered that First Mate Douglas take over the command of the ship. His first responsibility was to get a damage report, and it did not sound good.

"Sir, we have taken two major hits below the waterline in the forward compartment. We were able to contain one; however, the other one is too great and we cannot stop the flow," reported Mr. Douglas.

"How much time do we have?" asked the captain.

"Sir, I believe approximately thirty minutes." Mr. Douglas ordered all longboats lowered and told the crew to prepare to abandon ship. "Hopefully, the *Blackbird* will see our peril and pick everyone up." Mr. Douglas then gave the order to transport Captain Flowers and the other injured men to a longboat.

Barely able to speak, Captain Flowers said he would not leave and would go down with the ship. After hearing this, Thomas began to cry and wondered what his fate would be.

"No time to waste, lad," Captain Flowers whispered. "Take your cat and get in the longboat while you can. You'll be okay."

With the clock ticking fast, Thomas turned to get Barney, but he was not there. "Barney, where are you? Come here, Barney," called Thomas. The cat was nowhere to be seen, and the ship was starting to angle down slightly. "I've got to find him." Thomas began to panic. "Barney, Barney!" he shouted.

"Come, lad, we have to go now," said Mr. Douglas.

"No, I can't go until I have Barney cried Thomas!"

"You must, or you'll drown," said First Mate Douglas.

"No! I can't leave without Barney. I've just got to find him," said Thomas.

With his last dying breath, Captain Flowers told Mr. Douglas to get Thomas off the ship immediately.

Realizing this was Captain Flower's last command he grabbed Thomas by the hand and pulled him out of the cabin. As they fought their way down the ladder, Thomas shouted, "Barney, where are you?"

Thinking that Barney might have gone back to their original hiding place, Thomas suddenly pulled away from Mr. Douglas and ran to the ladder that went below decks. Rushing down the ladder and into rising knee-deep water, Thomas called, "Barney! Barney, where are you?" The water was rising extremely fast as Thomas made it to their original home. There, atop one of the barrels, was Barney. Looking relieved that Thomas had found him, Barney extended one of his paws. Crying and scared to death, Thomas reached out and grabbed Barney. The water was waist deep and the ship was filled with debris floating everywhere. As the water continued to rush in, Thomas fought to keep walking. While paddling with one hand and holding Barney with the other, Thomas made it back to within ten feet of the ladder. The water was now chest deep, making it almost impossible for Thomas to move. With only a few feet to go, it happened. The HMS *Provider* had given up, and was starting to take the final plunge to its resting place on the bottom of the ocean. As the sea poured into the hatch opening, Thomas was blinded by the rush of water.

Trying to hold Barney with one hand and the rail with the other, Thomas took one last breath of air as he tried to save himself and his cat. Kicking and paddling in total darkness, Thomas could only swim toward a ray of sunlight coming from above. After what seemed like forever, Thomas and Barney popped to the surface. Coughing and splashing, Thomas tried to hold on to anything that was floating. Barney, trying to do the same, spotted a large piece of floating bulkhead. Looking like a drowned rat, Barney crawled aboard. Totally exhausted, Thomas could only hold on to the side; he could not pull himself up. Adrift now among many pieces of floating debris from both ships, Thomas looked around expecting to see someone or one of the longboats nearby. Much to his surprise, neither one was there! Apparently, the time he had taken to locate Barney had allowed the longboats a chance to get away from the sinking ships and to move toward the *Blackbird*. Not having the strength to muster a shout, Thomas could only watch as the remaining survivors were picked up by the *Blackbird* in the distance.

Alone at Sea

As sunset approached, Thomas realized that he could not remain in the water any longer. Not being able to see at night was one thing, but dangling legs in shark-infested water was another. As Thomas assessed the situation, he noticed that several pieces of the rigging and rope were attached to the floating bulkhead where Barney sat. *If I can just secure a piece of rope, I'll have a way to pull myself aboard.*

Working with one hand while holding on with the other, Thomas was able to secure the rope. Now, the task of pulling himself up and out of the water would present a challenge. With waves splashing over his body, Thomas started pulling himself onto the floating bulkhead. Barney sat, looking as if to say, "You can do it, Thomas, you can do it!" Finally, with one last bit of strength, Thomas pulled himself on board and immediately collapsed. Lying facedown next to Barney, Thomas was completely exhausted.

Fighting to escape and stay alive for several hours had taken its toll. Thomas was totally spent and could only lie motionless as he tried to recover. Although not on a longboat, Thomas was thankful that he and Barney were still alive and out of the water. Little did they know that this would be their home for days to come.

The wooden bulkhead seemed to be floating well and had several pieces of the rigging and sails hooked to it. Thomas was able to pull most of the pieces aboard, and secured them to the raft as best he could. To make sure they would not roll off into the sea, Thomas tied a piece of the sail in a manner that allowed him and Barney to crawl under it for the night. Although completely exhausted, Thomas's adrenaline was still pumping. There was no way either one would get a good night's sleep tonight.

Sunrise came soon, and most of the debris had drifted away overnight. Thomas scanned the horizon, and the *Blackbird* was nowhere in sight. A very sad feeling came over Thomas as he thought about the death of Captain Flowers and the outcome of the crew.

Lucky to be alive, Thomas prayed for his friend Bobba Lucca and the crews of both the *Provider* and the *Blackbird*. Thirst and hunger had not come yet, but Thomas knew they would in due time. The only chance now for survival was for them to be picked up by a passing ship or be washed ashore on one of the many nearby islands. Both options came with risks. If picked up, what kind of ship would it be? Would it be the *Venture* or the *Blackbird*? A friendly ship or a pirate ship? Realizing how his luck had been running since he'd left England, Thomas thought the second option of being washed ashore would be the safest at this point, as long as the island had both fresh water and food. The odds of this were not good.

Drifting and alive, Thomas started a new day on the raft. As he sat looking at Barney, both knew the dire situation they were in. If they did not drift ashore somewhere or get picked up by a passing ship, this would be the place where they would die. What would his family think if they were found dead on a raft? So much to think about, but they must stay alive. Wondering how close they were to land, Thomas remembered Captain Flowers saying they could arrive in Tahiti in several days. However, the prevailing westerly winds were now blowing them in the opposite direction. *Oh, how I wish the* Blackbird *would show up*, Thomas thought.

After a restless night, Thomas watched as the sun rose over the South Pacific. Under any other circumstances, Thomas and Barney would have enjoyed floating on the raft in the beautiful blue-green water, but not today. Fortunately, the temperature and water were warm, so they didn't have to worry about freezing to death. What they did have to worry about was food and water.

If only we had one of Mom's good breakfasts, Thomas thought. It was midmorning and the sun was starting to beam down. The only way to keep from burning was to stay under a piece of the sail. Having not slept the night before and feeling the slight motion of the raft, Thomas drifted off to sleep.

Alone at Sea

Several hours passed before he awoke with a growling stomach and a dry mouth. *So much water and none to drink*, Thomas thought.

Another day had passed, and the winds and seas were dead calm. The sun was almost unbearable as both Thomas and Barney grew weaker. That afternoon, while Thomas and Barney lay dozing, they were awakened by something hitting the raft.

"Look, Barney, there's fish jumping everywhere!" said Thomas. Several even landed on top of the raft. Quick to respond, Thomas grabbed two of the largest fish before they could flip back into the ocean. Barney had captured one and had already started to eat. *It is not dried and salted, but if Barney can eat it, maybe I can as well*, Thomas thought. He pulled out his pocketknife and sliced a piece of the raw meat from the side of one of the fish. After rinsing it off, Thomas gave it a try. "Not bad, Barney," said Thomas, after he swallowed his first bite. The raw fish also soothed his parched mouth and throat. Thomas knew that the raw fish would at least keep him alive for a little while. Both were so hungry that Thomas ate one whole fish, and Barney ate a little less than half of another.

After finishing their first meal aboard the raft, Thomas discarded the fish remains over the side of the raft. Within minutes, Thomas and Barney were surrounded by sharks. As if waiting for their next meal, the sharks circled the raft. The thought of being eaten alive terrified Thomas. Although the fish had given both Thomas and Barney renewed strength, the need for water was growing critical.

That afternoon the wind started to pick up, and Thomas noticed storm clouds gathering. The rain came—and what a rain. The little pockets on the sail started to collect water. Thomas hurried to spread out the remaining fabric, and he and Barney drank the collected water in each little pocket. Just as soon as it started, the rain ended. Looking like two dogs—or, in this case, two cats—Thomas and Barney lapped up the remaining water.

Oh, how good that water tasted. As Thomas kneeled and gazed down at the pieces of sail and rigging, a thought came to mind. *If I can wedge a piece of this rigging to the raft and attach a piece of the fabric to it, I could sail this raft. Sailing is one thing, but how do I steer it?* Looking at the rigging, Thomas had a plan. "I'll take my knife and notch out one of the cracks at the end of the raft. I'll then notch out one of the boards and slide it into the crack. With a makeshift tiller handle, I can sail this ship, Barney!" said Thomas.

Pulling in additional fabric and rigging that was trailing behind their raft, Thomas began the task of making a sail and rudder. Realizing that he would not have the energy to work in the next day's hot sun, Thomas worked feverishly to complete his tasks. Starting with the rudder and then the mast, Thomas's carving skills now came into play. Working until dark, Thomas retired for the evening. Excited about what he had accomplished that day and thinking about this plan, Thomas experienced another almost sleepless night.

Although still thirsty and hungry, Thomas awoke with a renewed outlook. *If we have to eat fish and drink rainwater every day until we're found, so be it. Today is a new day, and I have lots of work to do.*

Before long, Thomas had just about completed the sail and rudder. While working on the final adjustments, Thomas thought back on the day when the *Provider* was first launched. This would be a special day as well. "What shall we call her, Barney?" Thomas asked. "How about naming her after you and the *Provider*? The Purr-vider it is," said Thomas with a grin. Barney looked at Thomas as if to say, "That's purr-fect!"

The winds were now up, and Thomas was ready to go. With a strong pull on the rope, the sail filled immediately, so much so that the raft tilted up on one side and the remaining pieces of wood slid off into the water. Thomas fought to gain control, but found himself sliding off as well. Using both hands to grab anything, Thomas released the rope that was holding up the sail. Hanging precariously on its side, the raft suddenly fell back to the ocean's surface. Relieved that it didn't flip over, Thomas and Barney hung on for dear life. Back in the shark-infested water, Thomas hurried to pull himself back on board. Barney used every claw on his paws to hold on.

Assessing the situation, Thomas discovered that he had lost most of the spare wood pieces and fabric. However, the makeshift mast and sail were still intact. To keep this from happening again, Thomas raised the sail very slowly to get a feel for how to sail the raft without turning it over again. With both himself and Barney situated, Thomas began to raise the sail. The strong wind immediately took hold, and the raft turned and started moving. Pulling up the sail to half mast, Thomas could feel the raft start to rise up on one side as it sliced through the water. Sensing a reoccurrence, Thomas shifted his weight to the rising side, which brought the raft back down. Getting a feel from the wind in the sails and leaning against the windward side of the raft, Thomas eased the sail straight up. The raft immediately responded and picked up speed. The faster they went, the more confident Thomas got.

Excitedly, he yelled, "Okay, Barney High Tail, let's go sail!"

Off they went, moving swiftly across the ocean, but to where? Without any navigational equipment, it would be very easy for them to sail in a circle, getting nowhere. However, Thomas did remember several things about the direction they were sailing before the *Provider* met its fate. The sun would always rise about amidships on the starboard (right) side and would set just off the larboard (left) bow. Thomas knew that under the best of circumstances it would be difficult to maintain this heading, but at least it would keep them from going in a circle. If this northwesterly tack could be maintained, with luck they might reach one of the many smaller islands that surround Tahiti.

Signs of Life and Death

Two days had passed, and both Thomas and Barney were growing weaker by the hour. Sunburned, hungry, and dehydrated, it was becoming more difficult for Thomas to stay focused. His hands raw from pulling on the rope that controlled the tiller, Thomas was getting very concerned. With the fabric draped over him and Barney, they looked more like a floating tent than a raft.

Late that afternoon, Thomas began thinking that he was starting to hallucinate. There before them floated three coconuts. Steering the raft as close as possible, Thomas was able to grab two, but did not risk trying to reach the third one. While trying to cut through the tough coconut shell, Thomas sliced his hand! This was not just a small cut; the knife penetrated all the way to the bone. The bleeding started slow, but soon was flowing freely down his arm. The dripping blood ran down through the planks of the raft and into the sea. Thomas knew this would draw the sharks, but more importantly, he needed to stop the bleeding, and fast. Tearing off a piece of the sail, Thomas was able to tie the salty wet cloth around his hand, which helped close the wound and slowed the bleeding.

Realizing that the coconut meat and milk could help keep them alive, Thomas worked feverishly to try and open the coconut. Opening a coconut with two good hands takes some skill, but trying to open one with an injured hand is almost impossible. Concentrating on boring out one of the coconut eyes, Thomas finally cut through the hard shell. Tilting the coconut up with excitement, Thomas began sucking like a newborn calf. He could not believe how good that coconut milk tasted. "Here, Barney, try some." Thomas poured a little into a pocket of the fabric. At first, Barney was reluctant, but knowing it was something other than salt water, he began to lap it up. Now, the task of opening the shell. While holding the empty coconut between his legs, Thomas raised the other coconut above his head and brought it crashing down against the other coconut. As luck would have it, the empty coconut split in half, exposing the beautiful white meat. "Barney, just imagine this coconut meat and milk is Mom's chicken and dumplings."

A third day had passed, and time was running out for both Thomas and Barney. Except for a small flying fish that ended up landing on the raft, there had been nothing more to eat or drink. Thomas tied off the rope that controlled the tiller and tried to get some sleep. Before nodding off, Thomas wondered if tomorrow would be their last. He prayed that it wasn't.

The sun was starting to rise on the fourth day, and Thomas was awakened by the sounds of seagulls. Squinting and rubbing his eyes, Thomas looked straight up and couldn't believe the number of seagulls. He had not seen that many since leaving Pitcairn Island. Could it be that they were near Tahiti?

Marooned

Four days adrift had left Thomas with dry, cracked lips, sunburned skin, and eyes that he could barely open. Barney had also suffered the effects. Barely able to move or open his salt-encrusted eyes, he lay next to Thomas, content in the closeness of his friend.

Thomas was resigned to the fact that, unless found, no one except Barney would ever know what had happened. Too weak to cry, Thomas thought he might never see his family again. Several hours went by as Thomas drifted in and out of consciousness.

Suddenly, a slight bumping was felt, as if the raft had hit something or had run aground. Without enough strength to raise his head, Thomas could only try to open his eyes. As he did, he wondered if he was awakening from a dream, or if this was heaven.

What appeared before them was one of the most beautiful sights he had ever seen. Before his eyes lay a tropical paradise! It might or might not be Tahiti, but it was land and a reason for hope! With the possibility of finding food and fresh water, Thomas rolled off the raft and into the warm shallows. Fighting to keep their heads above water, Thomas and Barney finally reached the shore. As Thomas squinted at the lush green jungle just ahead, it reminded him of a desert oasis. *Is it real or not?* He wondered. *So close, yet so far away.* It was taking every ounce of energy they had left to move. Every foot they crawled took total concentration, and Thomas wondered if it might be better to just stop and die there on the beach. "I can't, I can't," Thomas repeated. "Come on, Barney, we have to try. Just a few more feet and we'll be in the shade." Totally exhausted, Thomas and Barney finally made it to the edge of the jungle. While Thomas was looking up and feeling blessed that they were still alive, a tropical shower suddenly came. Opening his mouth to capture the raindrops, Thomas realized that he and Barney had a chance to live. As he pulled Barney close to his side, his thoughts turned to all that had happened. *This is not home, Barney, but its land and there's a reason to live. Tomorrow will be another day, and at least we have each other.*

About the Author

The path of life takes many turns and yes times as well. Having written his first book after retirement, author Henry Hixson realized that both paths of life and times are sometimes the best ingredients for a writer.

Henry has always loved people and the sea. After studies at the University of South Carolina in business and a stint in the U. S. Navy, Henry began a successful thirty-five year career in sales and marketing. Having retired early allowed him more time to spend with family and friends. Much of this time was spent telling stories to his grandchild, nephew, and niece. The enjoyment of storytelling and the love of the sea helped create The Adventures of Thomas Pilgrim and Barney High Tail. When not writing, you may find Henry enjoying a beautiful sunset on his dock on Edisto Island, S. C. Although his love of writing started later in life, Henry would be first to say "you're never too old to create a dream".

Made in the USA
Charleston, SC
23 April 2012